ROCKY MOUNTAIN REDEMPTION

ROCKY MOUNTAIN REVIVAL SERIES - BOOK 1

LISA J. FLICKINGER

WILD HEART
BOOKS

"Being justified freely by his grace through the redemption that is in Christ Jesus."

Romans 3:24

CHAPTER 1

1898

THE ROCKY MOUNTAINS

sabelle slid the moist length of potato peel between the thumb and forefinger of each hand and stretched her arms apart as it unfurled.

One handbreadth longer than yesterday's best. Six months ago, she couldn't have imagined being hidden away in a lumber camp and performing such tedious work.

Thanks be, the trembling in her fingers remained minimal. Doctor Bradley, a frequent visitor to Isabelle's second-story bedroom before she'd been dropped at the camp, had advised her parents the tremors would subside as she regained her health. It appeared he'd been correct.

Isabelle tossed the peel on the mound atop the long table serving as a work counter in the center of the kitchen and wiped her hands on the white muslin apron at her waist. The potatoes were a treat usually reserved for the weekends, a welcome break from the enormous iron pots of beans.

The logging camp's twenty-one men tucked away an

astounding volume of food Aunt Lou and Isabelle prepared and served every morning and every night. Why had Father thought such tedious work would cure what ailed her?

Isabelle dumped the peels into an enamel slop pail and wiped the counter. Aunt Lou didn't abide any mess in her kitchen, and Isabelle dared not leave one.

A quick jaunt to the creek and she could empty the slop pail while Aunt Lou slept in the small bedroom near the back door of the cook shack. She'd complained of sore joints earlier in the day, and Isabelle had urged the older woman take a short nap before the evening's meal preparation began in earnest. If Isabelle was quiet, Aunt Lou would be unaware of her niece's escape.

Isabelle snatched up the handle of the slop pail and tiptoed through the screened back door helping to keep the kitchen cool. As she scurried down the hard packed dirt toward the trees, Isabelle dared a look over her shoulder—no Aunt Lou.

Near the creek, tall pines cast long shadows on her path and the cool air of the forest enveloped her. She passed towering poplars and narrow birch trees, their leaves a bright patchwork of orange, gold, and brown. Spongy mosses cushioned the forest floor. A tangle of roots on the trail slowed Isabelle's pace.

She stopped and swung the pail, both hands on the handle, in a full circle. The pungent aroma of the pines coated the back of her throat like a balm. How could she have lived seventeen years without setting foot in such grandeur? Even her best friend and next door neighbor, Kittie, wouldn't understand when Isabelle tried to describe the hint of joy she felt among the trees, high on the mountain's side—if she ever saw Kittie again.

When Isabelle reached the creek, she leaned over the bank and tipped the pail above the bubbling water bedded with smooth, round rocks of vivid pink, dusty brown, and speckled gray. The peels floated on the surface and, drawn by the current, scattered downstream until they rounded the corner out of sight.

If only the overwhelming anxiousness stealing Isabelle's sleep hours before every dawn, would scatter and disappear like the peelings on the creek's surface.

Isabelle closed her eyes and inhaled another long, deep breath. An image of Daniel's intimidating face entered her mind, and her eyes popped open. She swallowed and tossed the bucket into the moss. Aunt Lou wouldn't know Isabelle was missing from the kitchen for another twenty minutes at least, plenty of time for Isabelle to soak her feet in the refreshing waters and try to forget about Daniel.

Isabelle twisted the hem of her navy skirt and white petticoat around her thighs. The cool air of the forest tickled her skin, and she shivered. Grasping a pliant willow to slow her descent, she turned and scooched down the steep, graveled bank. Halfway down, the smooth leather soles of her black boots turned on the damp stones, and she fell.

"Ouch!" Clamping her teeth together, she squeezed her eyes until the piercing pain under her hipbone subsided. It had been foolish not to remove her boots before descending the bank.

Isabelle sat up and plucked at the laces of her boots until they were loose before pulling them off and tossing them onto the path along the creek bank. Her wool socks soon followed. After descending the remaining incline, she slid her feet into the water. Her toes curled under at the chill.

Aunt Lou had informed Isabelle the creek never warmed, even in midsummer, due to the thick layers of snow at the higher elevations. The cool water provided storage for the milk; cream, and butter the men were so fond of.

As Isabelle bent and scooped a handful of water to slurp, a branch snapped on the bank. She whipped around and stepped back into the creek. Her hands shook, and the heavy folds of her clothing dropped into the water

"Is someone there?"

"Yes." The response came from a male voice.

Isabelle's heart lurched. Had she been followed? Aunt Lou had forbidden her to leave the cook shack unescorted. Why had Isabelle done it? She knew how risky taking chances could be.

"If you don't leave right now, I'll scream."

"All right...But I have a question first."

"You have a question before you leave or before I scream?"

"Both, miss."

Was he some kind of lunatic? The way the cold water had numbed her feet and calves, she would be fortunate if she could walk, let alone run, from an assailant. "What's your question?"

"Are you decent?"

"Am I decent?" Perhaps not a lunatic but a polite voyeur. Was there such a thing?

"It's just, well, when you scream, the men will come running, and if you're not decent, you'll regret it."

"Sir, do you have any idea how cold this water is?"

"I do. We men folk bathe in it when the scent in the bunkhouse is strong enough to curl the hair on your toes. Alvin usually puts up a fight, but the rest of us enjoy the brisk cleansing."

Isabelle shivered. Now that the man mentioned toes, she could no longer feel hers. Risky or not, she would have to leave the water. Lifting her water soaked skirt, Isabelle stepped toward the bank.

"You haven't answered my question."

She froze. Water trickled from her skirt into the creek. "Yes, I'm fully clothed. As a matter of fact, I wouldn't have stepped as deep into the water if you hadn't surprised me." Isabelle fixed her gaze on the bank where she'd descended. "Whoever you are."

"In that case." A head and broad shoulders appeared over the edge of the bank. The man wore a narrow brimmed hat, and reddish brown curls teased the collar of his checkered wool shirt. His dark blue eyes took in the length of her from under long full lashes.

He didn't look like one to take advantage, but she wasn't known to be a proper judge of character either.

The corners of his mouth turned up into a wide smile accenting the deep cleft in his chin.

Isabelle's shoulders twitched at his frank appraisal. If she didn't leave the water shortly, her feet would turn to ice.

"Who would have guessed?" the man said. "Snoop was telling the truth. There's been a lot of speculation. In fact, the men have been taking bets on whether another woman resides at the camp or not. Snoop swore he saw a tall slender woman with a braid down to her knees walking the moonlit path to the cook-house when he went to use the facilities last Thursday."

It was true. Isabelle's father had delivered her to the camp close to midnight the week before. He was still angry when they'd arrived and had merely stood at the carriage door and given her instructions on which path would lead her to Aunt Lou. With only the moon's glow to light her way, Isabelle had walked past a long, low cabin she assumed was the bunkhouse to an even longer log building with two small windows at the back. "I did arrive last Thursday"—Isabelle worried the nape of her neck as the man studied her—"but my hair was pinned up."

"I figured you were wishful thinking on Snoop's part until I heard you exclaim earlier. Did you hurt yourself?"

"No, I slipped on the rocks. You go back to the camp. I'll manage." The sooner the stranger left, the better. Isabelle needed time to wash her skirt and petticoat with the washboard in the kitchen before her aunt woke up. Otherwise, she would have to explain why her skirt was a sodden mess.

"Miss?" He raised a heavy eyebrow.

Isabelle dipped her chin as she replied, "Miss Isabelle Frank-lin, sir."

"Franklin? Are you a relative of the cook?"

"She's my father's sister."

Isabelle's stomach fluttered as the man's gaze slid over her from head to toe.

"I can't say as I see much resemblance."

Aunt Lou was as wide as Isabelle was narrow—and tall. She towered over Isabelle's five foot seven. Isabelle's father alleged that Aunt Lou had turned men's heads when she was a young woman. These days, she was as likely to knock them off as to turn them. The woman wielded a broom like a fiend. Since Isabelle's arrival, she'd clattered out of the kitchen twice to chase a logger from the dining room before meal time. And judging by the hollering that followed, she'd connected with at least one body part on each man.

With two leaps down the graveled bank, the logger landed by Isabelle's side in the creek. "Charles Bailey, otherwise known as Preach, at your service, Miss Franklin." He doffed the cap from his head, bent at the waist, and reached out a large calloused palm. "May I escort you up the bank? It would be impolite of me to leave you in danger of both man and beast."

The man was a giant. Even bent over he made an imposing figure. His black leather boots were almost twice the size of her own. Isabelle stared at his outstretched palm. Was the man dangerous?

He straightened his back and withdrew his hand. "Ah, cautious are you? I suppose I do appear daunting on first meeting."

Isabelle tipped back her head to meet his eyes.

He gathered his rough curls before he returned his cap to his head and snugged it down.

"Why are you called Preach?"

A low chuckle spilled from his chest. "An unlikely title, for certain. The men used to call me Bunyan." His grin revealed pearled, even teeth, except for one blackened bicuspid on the top jaw. "I'm sure you can guess why. As for the name Preach, at spring break-up this year, while celebrating the season's end in Stony Creek, I stumbled into a tent meeting by accident. The minister urged all those tired of the way they were living to come to the front and be prayed for. I *was* tired, tired of working hard and having nothing to show for it other than several weeks of carousing at the end of the season." Preach's neck turned a soft pink. "Pardon my rough talk, miss"

Isabelle nodded to encourage him to continue.

"So I went forward and cried like a little baby while the preacher prayed over me. The men say I'm different now." He cocked his head as though in contemplation. "I wish I were a whole lot different."

The same wish had jabbed at Isabelle's heart since May.

"In these parts, I'm the closest thing there is to a man of the cloth." He stretched out his hand once more. "So, would you permit me to escort you up the bank, Miss Franklin?"

If you couldn't trust a man named Preach, a man who loved the Lord, who could you trust? Isabelle gathered the folds of her skirt and reached out. His palm engulfed hers as he pulled her up the slope, over the embankment, and onto the path.

Toward them, broom at her side, lips pinched in a tight grimace, marched Aunt Lou. "Why am I not surprised? No more than a week at the camp and I find you cavorting in the woods with the men. I warned you not to leave the cook shack without me."

The accusation hit its mark. Isabelle snatched her hand from Preach's grip and dropped her chin. "I'm sorry, Aunt Lou," Isabelle's chest warmed, and she willed the crimson flush to remain below her collar. Regardless of her aunt's claim, Isabelle and Preach hadn't done anything improper.

"Your father led me to believe you were weak willed regarding men, and now I've seen it with my own eyes."

Weak willed regarding men? Isabelle had only ever been

courted by Daniel, and she and Father had never spoken of the relationship's demise, nor had Father ever asked to hear the particulars. Instead, he'd searched out numerous cures for her "ailment" and had finally resorted to hiding her away with her aunt at the logging camp.

Her cook's hat askew and her blue eyes snapping at Preach, Aunt Lou stopped at the creek bank's edge and raised the straw end of the broom in the air.

Preach stepped back into the moss, removed his cap, and lifted his large palm toward her. "Now, Lou, don't get yourself worked up."

Too late for that, Preach.

"The girl and I were not cavorting."

Isabelle glanced sideways at Preach, and he winked in return. Did he think the situation funny? There was nothing humorous about Aunt Lou when she was angry.

Aunt Lou poked the broom near Preach's face as he replaced his cap. "I can see what you were doing. Her skirt is soaking wet. When I tell Joe what you've been up to"—she thrust again —"he'll see you run off this camp, and I'll make sure you don't find work within a hundred miles."

Preach shouldn't lose his job at Pollitt's Lumber because of Isabelle's foolishness. "I'll go." Surely someone else would take her in. Perhaps Mother's cousin who lived further north "It's my fault, I wanted—"

"You, young lady, will be quiet."

"Aunt—"

Aunt Lou turned, and the broom whisked through the air toward Isabelle's shoulder.

Preach swung out, stopping the broom in its path.

Aunt Lou reared back, and her heel caught on a gnarled root. She stumbled backwards. Her arms flailed in the air, and she lost hold of the broom handle. Isabelle leaped forward to catch her, but the rough gray wool of Aunt Lou's skirt slipped through her fingers. Isabelle gasped as Aunt Lou slipped down the bank on her haunches before summersaulting backward and landing with a grand splash in the creek.

Isabelle and Preach rushed after her.

Aunt Lou plucked her cap from the cold water and tucked it on her wild gray ringlets. Rivulets streamed down her broad cheeks and nose.

Isabelle stifled the desire to giggle.

"When I am fit to deal with this matter, you will be sorry you ever tangled with me or my niece, Preach Bailey."

Preach's eyes twinkled and without a grunt he lifted Aunt Lou's large frame from the water and stood her upright at the water's edge.

"Now, Lou," he said, the deep timbre of his voice carrying a hint of amusement, "you know you don't mean it."

Aunt Lou swatted at Preach. "I do mean it. Move away from me, young man."

Isabelle looped her arm through her aunt's. "Are you hurt?"

Puffing her chest like an angry hen, Aunt Lou squared her shoulders. "Nothing more than a few scratches. I'll be quite fine. Help me up the bank, Isabelle. I'll go straight to the boss."

Preach removed his cap. His curls fell forward as he lowered his chin. "Lou, there's no need for you to speak to Joe. I promise you that Miss Isabelle and I had no knowledge of one another up until our meeting a few minutes before your arrival. And you and I both know Joe will be just as surprised as I was to discover an unmarried young woman at the camp."

Aunt Lou drew in a quick breath. "Why do you presume he doesn't know?"

"She arrived in the middle of the night. We've seen neither hide nor hair of her since then, and it's against the rules. No unmarried women at camp."

That explained why Aunt Lou forbade Isabelle to leave the area comprising the kitchen and two small bedrooms when the men were in the dining hall. It wasn't a punishment. It was necessary to keep Isabelle's presence hidden. "Aunt Lou, if I'm not allowed to be here, why did you offer to take me in?"

Aunt Lou raised her chin and sniffed. "Your father thought it was best. You were wasting away, and he feared for your life. We both thought the fresh air and hard work would help you to..."

Isabelle froze. The handsome giant before her didn't need to know why Isabelle was at the camp. *Please don't say it.*

Preach cocked his head and raised an eyebrow. His gaze carried a question, a question Isabelle hoped would not be answered.

"...find your way."

Isabelle exhaled with relief. *Find her way.* What a polite turn of phrase for the dark journey she'd experienced since the night of the May Ball, a journey that had threatened to crush the very life from her. Father's fear had been justified. Isabelle had no appetite for months as she'd hidden away from family, friends, even God, in her bedroom. Her clothes still hung from her as if they belonged to someone else.

"Let's get you back to the cook shack, Auntie." Isabelle urged her aunt up the incline. "We both need to find dry clothes."

Preach followed them up the slippery stones. "Are we agreed then, Miss Lou? You'll forgive me for my perceived indiscretion with your niece, and I won't tell Joe you've hidden a temptation away in the kitchen."

A temptation? Could a healthy, strong man like Preach be attracted to Isabelle, thin and pale as she was? She looked back at him. His face held no expression. Perhaps he was referring to how the other men at the camp would perceive her.

"I will only agree if you will not mention Isabelle's presence to anyone. As far as you're concerned, she does not exist."

They reached the top of the bank, and Preach held out his hand to shake Aunt Lou's. "Agreed."

She hadn't met Preach more than half an hour before, but the thought of him forgetting about her pricked Isabelle's heart.

Aunt Lou ignored Preach's outstretched hand as Isabelle retrieved her socks and boots. After motioning for Isabelle to precede her, Aunt Lou puffed her way down the path several steps before speaking. "Go on ahead and check the camp, Preach. See if it's clear for us to return. We need to finish preparing supper. You know how the men will grumble if it's late."

"Yes, ma'am."

As Preach passed Isabelle, the sleeve of his shirt brushed her shoulder. The path was wide enough to avoid the encounter. Perhaps, as far as Preach was concerned, Isabelle did exist.

Isabelle stepped from the path to fetch the pail from the moss and then fell in behind her Aunt's wide back to continue toward the cook shack. Before they left the cover of the forest, Preach waved a signal—all was clear.

The door of the kitchen shack had barely squeaked closed before Aunt Lou barked out orders. "Remove your wet things immediately, young woman, and put them in the washtub. You will scrub all of our garments after supper. And while you do, think about the trouble you've caused. A little more thought for others, and you wouldn't be in the predicament you're in."

"Why didn't you tell me it was against the rules for me to work at the camp? If I'd have known I—"

"Why didn't you do what you were told to do?"

Perhaps Aunt Lou was right. Isabelle hadn't listened to her parents in the weeks preceding the May Ball. And now that she was at the camp, her misbehavior had caused Preach trouble, too.

"After you've changed," Aunt Lou said, "see the table is set and then return to the kitchen. We've some apple pies to make before supper."

"Yes, ma'am."

Ten minutes later, dressed in a plain cotton dress with tiny blue flowers, Isabelle set one enameled plate and mug after another on a clean, white oilcloth. Twenty-one men would assemble around the half-log table lining the center of the windowless dining room. The structure was built of logs with moss stuffed in the gaps to keep out the chill. Although the floor was rough sawn lumber, Aunt Lou insisted it be swept spotless morning and night.

After setting the table, Isabelle rolled out pastry for ten pies before mixing a batch of bread for tomorrow's lunches. Aunt Lou kept busy preparing beef hash, mashed potatoes, carrots, and stewed prunes for the evening meal. She served the men's supper alone while Isabelle hid in the kitchen, nibbling at the food on her own plate.

After supper, Isabelle and Aunt Lou washed the dishes before making sugar cookies, molasses cookies, and a pound cake. Isabelle washed their clothes and hung them to dry next to the double cook stove dominating the kitchen before gathering the lamps from the dining room.

With a soft piece of cotton, she polished each lampshade to a shine. The day had finally come to an end, and Isabelle could hardly keep her eyes from fluttering to a close. Perhaps Father had been right. The unaccustomed chores left little time to dwell on the past.

Her heart quickened as she remembered Preach's strong jaw and dimpled chin, the way he'd grasped her hand in his own large one to help her from the creek. The way he'd protected her from Aunt Lou's broom, with no fear in his eyes, warmed her to her center. More than likely, Aunt Lou would make sure the improbable preacher didn't cross Isabelle's path again.

CHAPTER 2

$\mathcal{M}$oisture filled the bunkhouse from the wet clothes hanging from cross-shaped poles above the stove.

Preach rolled the piece of dry aspen on his palm and drew the tip of his knife blade down the bend of one carved wing. It created a fine curl which fell to the rough sawn floor and collected with the other shavings. Forcing his shoulders back, he arched his spine to stretch out the kinks and cracked his neck from side to side. The thirty-foot bunkhouse was warm, too warm. Perley had thrown several logs in the stove minutes before. Sitting in the heat after a hearty meal of beef hash and potatoes followed by apple pie, Preach's energy waned.

Lou had been her usual, ornery self at supper, and Preach hadn't managed one peek of Isabelle. Not that he had expected one, but a man could hope. He wouldn't have known about Isabelle's presence at the camp if he hadn't come in early to meet with Joe and go over some figures in the office. Ever since he'd met the sweet little thing, she'd been on his mind.

Lou had stopped Preach short when he'd offered to refill the water jug from the pail in the kitchen. She'd snatched the jug from his grip and muttered something about keeping his word if he knew what was good for him.

The meal had been a silent one, as usual—boss's orders. It kept the men from bragging and fighting during the meal. Whenever the men compared log counts for the day, there was no end to the arguments, and it usually ended up with one of the lumberjacks sporting a black eye worth writing home about. There was no fighting in the bunkhouse either. All fisticuffs were decreed to happen out of doors.

"Preach, you going to stop your moping in the corner and come and join the game?" Will yelled from the far side of the bunkhouse where he, Horace, Perley, and Mack sat on narrow half-log benches around a crudely built round table.

Preach wasn't brooding. He hadn't felt this hopeful in months. "You boys go ahead. Perley's got the bunkhouse so warm I can barely keep my eyes open."

Preach rose from the edge of his bunk and crossed the floor to open the door of the bunkhouse several inches. It would help with the heat and the ripe scent tearing at his nostrils. The men would have to wrangle Alvin down to the creek before long.

Preach smiled at the memory of Lou rolling down the bank and making a splash. It would've made for a good story in the bunkhouse if he could tell it.

"You know, Preach," Snoop said to Preach's back, "watching you handle that purty little sparrow you've been whittling, I'd almost swear you were love sick."

Preach's hand stilled on one of the thick, pine slabs of the bunkhouse door. Snoop could ferret out a story from even the smallest of details. Preach laughed, hoping it sounded natural, before turning to face his fellow logger. Shirtless, scars criss-crossing his chest, the whip-thin man reclined on his bunk mending a wool sock.

The trick was not to let Snoop know he might be on to something. Preach stared Snoop straight in the eye before speaking. "Are you surmising I found your wood nymph from the other night?"

Snoop glared right back. "Did ya?" he asked, his brown eyes daring Preach to lie.

"You mean that short, hairless woman you claimed to see in the dark when you were half asleep?" *Forgive me, Isabelle, but I did promise your Aunt Lou.*

"That's not what I said," Snoop snarled, "and you know it."

"Pretty sure it was, Snoop." Will, the youngest man in the bunkhouse, joined the conversation. "I recall distinctly. You said you saw a wee thing with her hair all shorn dancing near the cook shack. She was carrying a lantern and whistling."

Whistling?

"I remember, too," his bunkmate Mack piped up. "Only, there wasn't just one of them, there were twenty—one for each of us."

The other men in the bunkhouse began hooting and jeering. Some of them called out even more bizarre descriptions of the women they hoped existed.

"I know what I saw." Snoop turned his back to the others and continued his mending.

Thank you, boys. That should keep Snoop off the scent for a long while.

Preach returned to his bunk and picked up the sparrow sitting in a nest he'd been carving since he returned to camp in the fall. It was almost finished. Running his thumb across the beak and over its head, he traced the finely detailed feathers. This was some of his best work. Ever since he'd been prayed for, he didn't have the same desire to spend his money playing cards or betting on the latest wager Perley offered up.

If only Preach could say the same about his other desires. Isabelle's milky white calves came to mind, and his heart picked up its beat. What she and Lou didn't know was that he'd been watching Isabelle from a bend in the creek while she'd soaked her feet. He'd gone down to fetch one of the sarsaparillas he kept chilling in the cool water before meeting with Joe when he'd seen Isabelle standing in the stream, skirt hiked up around her knees. As she stood, head back, eyes closed, and lips moving soundlessly, the curve of her long neck had brought to mind another neck, where Preach had trailed kisses and pushed back long tresses to nuzzle the hollow behind an ear. The vision of Isabelle was one he would not soon forget.

Forgive me, Lord. Isabelle deserves better than these coarse thoughts of mine. He looked at the nest in his palm. *She's one of yours, Lord, and You care for her like you care for each sparrow.*

Preach dropped his knife into his pocket and slid the sparrow and nest under the end of his bunk before shedding his over-clothes and climbing under the red woolen blanket. Horace would make sure the lanterns were snuffed out at nine o'clock. Preach's eyelids drooped. He couldn't keep them open much longer. After folding the blanket to his waist, he rolled onto his good shoulder. The spruce boughs he'd woven into a spring mattress snapped under his weight. He rolled back onto his spine and sighed.

"You're doing a fair bit of fidgeting over there, Preach," Snoop said from his perch three bunks over. "You got a guilty conscience?"

Sure Preach did, but it had nothing to do with not telling Snoop his wood nymph was real.

Preach had promised Lou he wouldn't tell the men about Isabelle, and that was the part of the promise he would keep. There was no way he could pretend she didn't exist. Perhaps in time, Lou would trust him and he could pursue a relationship with her niece.

"You're seeing intrigue where there isn't any, Snoop. Better get some sleep."

"There's something going on all right," Snoop muttered under his breath. "I just haven't figured out what it is—yet."

"Good night. The morning's coming early." Preach yawned and turned back to his good shoulder.

Lord, it says in your word "it is better to marry than to burn." You know I've been praying about finding a wife, an innocent woman to lend me some respectability. I never expected to find a possibility so close by. If You could see to it that Lou gives me a chance with Isabelle it would be much appreciated.

⁓

*P*reach whipped the hat from his head and swiped at the sweat coursing down his forehead. The sun hadn't shown itself from behind the clouds the entire day, but his shirt had been soaked with sweat within a half hour of cutting. Mack hadn't spoken a word since they'd begun the trek home through the woods. Normally, the boy wouldn't stop talking. He'd started complaining of achy muscles before noon, and Preach had figured he was just whining. Mack liked to get away with doing less than his partner if he could, which was one of the reasons Preach had paired with him a couple of weeks into the season.

As foreman, Preach liked to work with the young'uns so they could learn how to cut without getting beat like Preach had been beat when he first started in the woods. Mack had tried Preach's patience more than most their first week together before he figured out Preach wasn't going to let him get away with not pulling his own weight. It was worrisome that the boy wasn't the usual chatterbox.

"You feeling any better?" Preach asked.

"Nope." Mack swayed on his feet before resting his back against a tree and sucking in two deep breaths.

Preach reached toward Mack. "Let me carry your tools."

Mack surrendered his axe, wedge, sledgehammer, and saw

with slow awkward movements. "I think I'm feeling worse, Preach." The words came out in a rush.

Five minutes later, they came to the main road. Alvin was skidding a log with Beauty, one of the camp's mares. Joe had changed her name after she'd tangled with a cougar and survived. She still bore the scars, deep grooves starting at her withers and crossing her flank. Alvin smacked the reins against Beauty's back as he nodded to Preach and Mack. His upper lip scrunched when he noted Preach carrying Mack's equipment.

"Hold up, Alvin. Mack's not feeling well. You think Beauty would mind if he caught a ride back to the camp."

"Whoa," Alvin said, and the horse slowed to a stop. "You look poorly, son. Let me drop this log." Alvin unclipped the traces from Beauty's collar, allowing the whiffletree to drop to the ground.

Preach helped Mack onto the horse and rolled the reins before handing them up to him.

Alvin pushed his scotch cap back from his eyes. " I've been meaning to ask you if Joe was having some of the log piles scaled already."

Unless he was tight for money, Joe didn't have his logs counted until spring. "He hasn't mentioned anything, why?"

"I saw a fellow measuring our piles the other day. He seemed surprised to learn the logs were Pollitt's and asked me about Thorebourne Timber. I sent him on his way."

The Thorebourne family, owner of the neighboring lumber company, was well off, but rumor had it the women liked to spend money. Mr. Thorebourne could be arranging for a prepayment on his harvest. "Perhaps Thorebourne's fallen on hard times."

"Ya, maybe."

Mack nudged the horse, and Beauty took several strides before her rider toppled over sideways and onto the ground.

Alvin and Preach ran to Mack's side.

Mack rolled over and groaned, his eyes squeezed shut.

"You alive?" Alvin asked.

"Barely," Mack groaned again. "Preach, I'm going to need your help."

Alvin and Preach maneuvered Mack into the saddle before Preach pulled himself up behind Mack, and they started for camp. The clang of Alvin's sledge hammer as he removed the U shaped metal dog he used for hauling pine logs followed them.

Mack remained slumped against Preach's chest for ten minutes, even though the horse stumbled in the deep ruts and on the sharp rocks of the poor road.

"Mack, you sleeping?"

The boy roused and muttered something about his ma's chicken soup before collapsing again.

Another fifteen minutes passed before Preach and Mack were back at the camp. Preach steered the horse toward the bunkhouse. Will, Perley, Snoop and several others milled around a small bonfire waiting for the supper bell, most likely talking about the day's harvest.

Mack hadn't stirred for a while.

"Will, Perley, help me get Mack in the bunkhouse. The boy's taken sick."

The men hurried toward the horse and riders.

"Take his feet, I'll hold him under the arms," Will said.

Mack lifted his head and muttered "What?" before his head lolled to the side.

Perley shifted his grip on Mack's feet. "You'll be all right, Mack. It's nothing a shot of whiskey and a good night's sleep won't fix."

Nobody knew if what Perley said was true, but hearing it calmed the others. They carried Mack to his bunk and stripped off his sweat-soaked clothes before covering him with his blanket. Mack's high fever and the rash blotching his cheeks reminded Preach of an outbreak they'd had years earlier at a rival camp.

Preach pawed through the breeches and Mackinaws in the locked supply box in the corner of the bunkhouse looking for another blanket to keep the chill off of the boy. Joe might complain about using new merchandise, but, if he had to, Preach would pay for it with his own earnings.

He scraped the bottom of the box as he grabbed the last blanket. There should have been several more in the box. Maybe Joe had taken a couple and forgotten to mention it. Preach would have to ask him about the blankets later.

"Will," Preach said, "go and tell the boss Mack's sick. I'll talk to Lou, see if she has any tablets to help with the boy's fever."

Will rushed out of the bunkhouse.

After Preach covered Mack with the extra blanket, he sprinted down the path and past the dining hall to the back door of the kitchen shack. With a curled fist he rapped twice before calling out, "Lou, it's Preach. Open up."

No one opened the door and walked in to Lou Franklin's kitchen without permission. The last man who had tried it had a dipper full of hot water from the reservoir thrown at him. The only remorse Lou had shown for the blisters on the man's cheek came in the form of camphor oil to the bunkhouse later that evening.

The door creaked open six inches. The light from the kitchen lanterns accentuated Isabelle's heart-shaped face and pretty brown eyes. A smudge of flour crossed one of her delicate cheekbones. She was just as beautiful as she'd been in his dreams the night before.

Preach reached out two fingers to swipe the flour from her cheek. She stepped back, and he swiped the air.

Good move, Preach. What were you thinking? She doesn't even know you. "Sorry, I was just going to"—he rubbed at his own cheek—"you have some flour right here."

Isabelle turned her head to the side before brushing her long fingers across her cheek, smearing the flour even more.

"I was hoping to see Lou."

Isabelle smiled, and once again her full lips brought to mind others—soft, pliant. His heart did a little jig.

"I'm sorry to disappoint you, Mr. Bailey. But Aunt Lou is indisposed."

"Where is she?" His voice sounded harsher than he'd meant it to. Why did the girl stir up such feelings in him?

"As I said, she's indisposed."

Enough of the time wasting, Preach. Keep your wits about you.

"Tell her I need to speak to her, *now.*"

Isabelle flinched at his raised voice.

Preach's belly knotted at her reaction. It was no way to treat a girl you intended to woo. "I'm sorry, I didn't mean to yell. Would you find Lou for me?"

"She left just after you and the men did. She and Joe went down the mountain to Stony Creek. They were doing the mail run and picking up kitchen supplies." Isabelle jutted out one hip and folded her arms. "I was under strict orders not to open this door for any reason."

He lowered his lashes to half mast, taking in her pretty face once more—flour and all. "And yet you did," he said softly.

Isabelle cast her gaze past his shoulder.

Preach stuck his boot against the base of the door to prevent its closure. "I need your help."

"My help? Aunt Lou said—"

"One of the boys, Mack, is near delirious with fever. I think he might have come down with hand, foot, and mouth. If I'm right, it won't be long before the whole bunkhouse will be down with it. I was hoping Lou might stock some fever tablets."

"If you let me close the door, I'll check the medical supply box in Aunt Lou's room. What else will you need?"

Preach pulled his boot back to the packed dirt. "Probably a

couple of pails of fresh water, to keep the men hydrated. I'll send Will down to the creek. Other than that, not much we can do. It's not fatal, but the men will be uncomfortable for close to a week. We had an outbreak eight years ago when I was working over at Svedberg's. Every one of us was down with the disease."

Isabelle closed the door.

It would have been warmer to wait inside, but it was best not to get her into further trouble with Lou. The evening's chill had long since seeped through his sweaty clothes and was threatening to freeze up his bones. Preach rubbed his hands together to bring the heat back into them.

Rustling and rattling emanated from inside the cook shack for several minutes before the door opened and Isabelle passed through two buckets. Each held several soft cloths and a couple of cups. One held the clear bottle of tablets he'd requested.

Preach slid his hand over Isabelle's to take the pails.

Jerking back, she gasped and the pails almost fell from both their grip. "I'm sorry," she said, whisking her long braid from behind her shoulder and worrying the frayed end.

Snoop had been exaggerating. The thick braid would only reach to Isabelle's waist—her tiny waist.

"It's all right," he said in a soothing tone. "It looks like you've gathered everything I need. I'll head back to the bunkhouse."

"Do you think the men will want their supper? It's warming in the oven. Aunt Lou should be back soon to put it on."

"Hard to say how many of the men will have taken sick. I'll check the bunkhouse and let you know."

"All right, then." Isabelle nodded and closed the door.

Preach turned with the pails to head to the bunkhouse. The girl was skittish, more skittish than any he'd ever met. But it wasn't as if she could read his mind. She had no idea what the sight of her did to his insides. Or did she? Preach's cheeks burned at the thought.

She was scared. That's why she'd jumped the way she had. Preach frightened her. Her hands had been shaking when he'd surprised her in the woods, too. Maybe it was his size. He couldn't blame her. He was a giant next to her slight form. He'd have to be gentler. Isabelle didn't need any more grief than he'd already brought her.

Lord, help Isabelle not fear me.

Perhaps she'd like a token. A bit more defining of the feathers, and the sparrow in the nest would make a perfect gift. Preach increased his pace. If there weren't too many down in the bunkhouse, he could finish the sparrow and sneak back to the kitchen without Lou's knowledge.

He slung the pails to one arm and opened the door. Four of the bunks were occupied with men wrapped up in blankets. Horace and Alvin sat hunched near the stove.

Sweet Isabelle wouldn't be getting any gift tonight.

CHAPTER 3

*I*sabelle bent and scooped two pails of water from the creek. Her frequent visits down the trail no longer held any joy. The trips had lost their appeal about halfway through the third day of the outbreak. Preach had been correct —the men had come down with hand, foot, and mouth disease, owing to the poor hygiene of a handful of the lumberjacks and the close quarters in the bunkhouse.

The night the men had taken ill, Aunt Lou had arrived shortly after Preach had left the kitchen door with the very buckets Isabelle was now filling. A good thing too. Aunt Lou had given several explicit warnings about not opening the door to anyone while she and Joe Pollitt, went for the supply run. She'd singled out Preach in her warning, claiming she hadn't liked the look in the man's eye when she'd come upon him and Isabelle at the creek earlier in the day.

If Isabelle's heart hadn't almost thumped out of her chest when she'd realized she wasn't alone at the creek, perhaps she might have noticed the yearning look Aunt Lou spoke of. Other than brushing by her sleeve, most likely by accident, Preach had been the perfect gentleman when she'd met him in the woods.

Nor had he done anything untoward since. And why would he? The man knew the Lord.

Isabelle would check the wood pile by the back door of the cookhouse when she returned. Preach had hidden a letter for her under a log each day since the start of the outbreak and Isabelle had replied to every one. He was an engaging writer, and shared tales about life in the woods and life on the farm. His love for the Lord, his fellow loggers, and the people of Stony Creek shone through in his words. He'd also asked after Isabelle and she'd been surprised by how easy the stories of her happy childhood, work with poor in Seattle, and service at her home church had fallen from her lips in spite of the secrets which had brought her to the camp.

At the end of every letter he had enclosed a brief prayer for her, and she'd hidden the notes in her room under the mattress.

Isabelle stared at the rocks lining the creek bed, all loggers were not as coarse or desperate as Aunt Lou made them out to be.

As Isabelle trudged with the buckets over the dank soil of the path toward the cook shack, birds flitted overhead from the needled boughs of one pine to another, oblivious to the chaos within the camp. Every few steps, water sloshed over the bucket rims, adding to the dampness of Isabelle's skirt and petticoat.

Better wet skirts than a mouthful of blisters and an itchy rash on her hands and feet. Some of the men were suffering terribly from the same rash on their nether regions as well. No one was certain why delirium had taken a hold of Mack. The others suffered only mild fevers.

According to Aunt Lou, no cure existed for the ailment. Preach and a man named Snoop, the only two still healthy by the morning after the outbreak, were keeping the ailing men hydrated with Isabelle's buckets of water, which Aunt Lou delivered to the bunkhouse door. They also swabbed the men's mouths with honey to help with the blisters.

Other than hauling water, tasks in the kitchen had almost come to a standstill, as the ailing men had no appetite. Aunt Lou also delivered meals to Preach and Snoop three times a day mumbling that she could feed five people in her sleep.

Isabelle plunked the buckets on the ground outside the kitchen door and checked the wood pile—no letter yet. "Aunt Lou," she called, stepping over the plank threshold. "Two more for you. Are you sure you don't want me to run them over?"

Aunt Lou looked up from the sheaf of notepaper on the counter next to a Zephyr Cream Sodas tin and laid the fountain pen down before smoothing the gray braid wrapped in a tight tower on the top of her head.

Writing again? Aunt Lou wasn't known as an avid correspondent. Isabelle's family only ever received an obligatory Christmas note saying little more than "hoping all is well" and "best wishes for the New Year."

"No more than I did an hour ago, young lady," she said, wiping her hands down the starched muslin apron around her waist, a gesture she used whether they were soiled or not.

"Preach already knows I'm here, and the rest, except for Snoop, are bedridden. It'll save you some steps on your 'old feet.'"

"It's Snoop I'm worried about. The boy couldn't keep a secret if he was paid to."

"Why do you continue to keep me hidden? I've met Preach," *and gotten to know and admire him,* "he doesn't seem like a bad sort. Perhaps the others—"

"You don't know what I know, and furthermore, the boss said no unmarried women at the camp, let alone one as young as you."

"You're unmarried."

"Something else I haven't been advertising, but the boss knows. I've been cooking in his camp for eight years, and I've never been any trouble." She glared over the top of her wire-rimmed reading spectacles. "I expect you to behave as well."

After collecting the papers and returning them to the tin, Aunt Lou tucked the tin under a sack of oatmeal on the supply shelf. "There's not much to do. We'll make a couple of mince-meat pies later this afternoon—Preach's favorite." Tipping her chin up, Aunt Lou observed Isabelle from the corner of one eye as though judging her reaction.

Isabelle settled her features into a smooth veneer. Preach's favorite pie was mincemeat, a good thing to know. Thanks to Aunt Lou, Isabelle could now make a pie in less than ten minutes. "Until then?" Isabelle asked.

"You can do some reading, if you like. I noticed you brought a fair bit of material with you."

Why was Aunt Lou going through Isabelle's personal belongings? Was her room not private? What if she found the letters?

"Did your father give you the impression you would have a lot of free time while you stayed with me?"

"He gave me no impression at all," Isabelle said. "In fact, he didn't say a word for the entire trip until he told me which shack I was to find you in."

"Humph."

"I heard he and Mother arguing shortly after supper the day Archie and he drove me up here. I couldn't hear what it was about, though. About half an hour later, my mother came to my room and cried as she packed my belongings. I'd taken to my bed with a headache that afternoon and missed my supper." Something that had occurred more often than not. "Mother wouldn't tell me what was happening. I suppose my father didn't know what to do with me." Worrying the end of her braid she lifted her gaze to her Aunt's. "It's understandable. For the most part, I don't know what to do with myself."

"Perhaps staying here will help you figure it out. Don't jeopardize the opportunity by being foolish."

A word used to describe Isabelle's behavior so many times in the last months, she'd stopped caring. "I'll be in my room when you need me."

Isabelle unlatched the door to her sleeping quarters as Aunt Lou bustled past to deliver the water. The tiny room, tucked by the back door, was opposite Aunt Lou's matching quarters. The room held a single bed, fashioned from rough lumber, with a straw mattress covered in striped ticking. On the bed lay a thick feather quilt Aunt Lou had sown from bits of gray and brown wool, most likely fragments of worn women's dresses and men's slacks. Below a three-paned window high in the wall, a narrow desk served as a catchall for her wash basin, toiletries, and books. Pegs driven into the exterior log walls held her skirts, blouses, and petticoats. Although the pegs were convenient, sap from the oozing logs had left patches of amber crust on several pieces of her clothing.

Closing the door, Isabelle glanced out the window toward the green of the forest. Aunt Lou couldn't keep her hidden in the cook shack forever. Although, the fact that Isabelle had been at the camp close to two weeks and Preach was still the only one to find out was owed to Aunt Lou's vigilance in supervising Isabelle's every movement—other than the trips to the creek.

A smile played at the corners of Isabelle's mouth as she remembered Aunt Lou's tumble into the water the afternoon Isabelle had met Preach. Aunt Lou would be horrified to discover the white of her bloomers had peeked from the folds of her skirt as she'd rolled down the bank. Most likely, Preach's bulged eyes as Aunt Lou landed with a splash indicated he'd been subjected to the same spectacle as Isabelle. It was a marvel and a blessing Aunt Lou hadn't been hurt.

Isabelle rested a finger atop the three stacked novels she was reading simultaneously and traced a circle on the rough buckram cover of *The Prisoner of Zenda*, the lighthearted read she'd brought to boost her mood when she became maudlin. Cooper's *Pathfinder* never disappointed in lulling her to sleep, and *Studies in the History of the Renaissance* kept her faculties from turning to mush.

At Mother's insistence, Isabelle had also packed her Bible. The beautifully tooled brown leather King James Version, a gift for her sixteenth birthday, remained unread, as it had since the spring.

Isabelle snatched up the top novel in the stack. Today's welcome respite from kitchen chores called for more of King Rudolf's adventures. After climbing on the bed and tucking the soft quilt around her knees, Isabelle flipped to the fourth chapter.

Several pages into her reading, she heard a light tap on the bedroom window. Glancing up, Isabelle could see nothing but blue sky and the tops of the trees at the edge of the clearing. Most likely one of the squirrels was up to its tricks again. They threw pine cones from the roof of the cook shack onto the stack of cut firewood. Occasionally, one of the pinecones bounced and struck one of the window panes.

Isabelle looked down at the page but had only read a line when two more taps, in quick succession, sounded on the window. It wasn't squirrels. She crossed the room and peered out.

Preach? Why was he being so bold?

Hands behind his back, a day's worth of growth on his cheeks, Preach stared back at her. His eyebrows arched as though hopeful.

Isabelle was in enough trouble with Aunt Lou already. If she discovered Isabelle had continued to communicate with Preach, Aunt Lou would demand Isabelle leave. She couldn't jeopardize the blossoming relationship with Preach. Isabelle shook her head, "No."

Preach pointed to the door.

Aunt Lou might be back any moment. Isabelle shook her head again.

Preach smiled and shifted from one foot to the other.

Why was he being so—"Oh."

Preach had brought one hand from behind his back. In his palm rested the carving of a small bird sitting in a nest. Although without color, the flawless shape and tilt of the bird's head made it look as though it were watching her.

Isabelle pointed at her chest. "For me?" she mouthed.

Preach jerked his chin in agreement.

Isabelle sprinted to the back door. "Where's Aunt Lou?" she whispered through the narrow opening.

"She's in the bunkhouse helping Snoop. I didn't get any sleep last night. She said I looked like death warmed over and sent me over to the boss's quarters early. I wanted to give you this first."

Isabelle opened the door and took the figure from him. The delicate nest followed the curves of her palm. Although all in one piece, it looked like interwoven twigs. She ran her finger across the bird's head and down its back. The fine marks on the body gave the feathers a realistic texture. The carving was exquisite. "You carved this? It's such fine work."

Preach rubbed the back of his neck. "For a big oaf like me, you mean."

Isabelle glanced up. "That's not what I meant." She dropped her gaze to the tiny bird. "It's so detailed, it looks real."

"It's a sparrow."

"I can tell."

Preach cleared his throat. "I've been working on it since we came out to the bush. It helps me..."

Isabelle looked back up to search his expression. "It helps you what?"

"Uh." He shrugged. "It helps me to avoid thinking about things."

Like reading kept Isabelle from replaying the night of the May dance over and over in her mind. "I know what you mean."

He cocked his head in question.

"You're not the only one with thoughts you want to avoid." Isabelle looked at the bird in her palm. She couldn't resist and petted its tiny head once more. "Thank you, but I don't think I should keep it. You've put so much work into it. It's beautiful." The precious bird should be given to someone important in his life. As she extended the nest toward Preach, she glanced up and saw that his brows were pulled into a tight furrow. "There's no one else you'd like to give it too?"

He shook his head.

No woman in his life who would appreciate such a lovely gift? The knowledge caused her stomach to warm.

"I want you to have it. Please." His large palm, fingers spread, stretched toward her. "I didn't know when I was carving it who it was meant for, but when I met you, I knew. It reminds me of you."

"The sparrow reminds you of me?"

Preach's cheeks colored a deep red as his Adam's apple bobbed. "Well, the verse in the Bible. Do you know the one?"

"Fear ye not therefore, ye are of more value than many sparrows?"

Preach nodded as Aunt Lou's screech cut through the air from the path around the cabin.

Isabelle yanked the door shut. It was as if Aunt Lou had a sixth sense when it came to Isabelle and Preach.

"Open that door!"

Isabelle stepped outside, balancing the nest in her palm.

Aunt Lou approached Preach and Isabelle, arms pumping like a soldier's, fury twisting her features. "Why am I not surprised? I figured I should come and see what the two of you might be up to."

Preach rubbed the side of his cheek, exhaustion etched on

his features. He faced Aunt Lou as she stomped up the path. "We're not up to anything, Lou. I'm going to get some shut eye." He stepped into the moss on the side of the path to circumvent Aunt Lou.

She grabbed his arm and yanked. "Not so fast."

As Preach hesitated, the cords in his neck pulsed above the collar of his shirt. He looked down at her grip on his bicep.

"Let go, Aunt Lou. We were simply talking."

"If you were *simply talking*, then what's this?" In two strides, Aunt Lou reached Isabelle and swiped out with the back of her hand. The nest in Isabelle's palm fell to the dirt path. As it landed, the sparrow's tail snapped in two places. The bird separated from the nest and rolled into the moss.

The orb of one sparrow eye stared up at Isabelle helplessly. She dropped to her knees. "How could you?" Isabelle plucked the broken pieces from the ground.

There had been no reason for Aunt Lou to break the gift. It was the sweetest thing someone had done for Isabelle in a long time. She looked at the fragments. Perhaps she and the sparrow were even more alike than before, both broken bits of something that had once been whole. Isabelle sniffed. She'd save the crying for later.

"Lou," Preach's tone held a warning, "that wasn't necessary."

"To you or to me? I told you earlier, as far as you're concerned. Isabelle does not exist. I expected you to listen."

"What are you so afraid of?" he asked.

"The last thing this girl needs is some sweet talking savage sweeping her off her feet and leaving her with a young one to care for."

Isabelle sucked in a ragged breath. Had her ears deceived her?

"Your words are an insult to both your niece and myself."

No, they weren't. The heat built in Isabelle's chest as she stood and brushed the soil from her skirt.

Aunt Lou huffed. "It's not without reason her father sent her to the camp to stay with me. The girl's tainted."

Preach's silence indicated he understood Aunt Lou's implication. Isabelle closed her eyes. If only she could crawl into a hole, a dark hole, and never come out.

Several long moments passed.

"Nevertheless," Preach said, "Isabelle deserves your apology. We weren't doing anything immoral."

"An apology? An apology is not something she will be getting from me. You go back to the bunkhouse. It appears you weren't as tired as I'd thought." Aunt Lou's skirts nearly toppled Isabelle as she whisked by her niece toward the cook shack door. "Isabelle, come inside."

Preach picked up the pieces of the bird. "You keep the nest," he said, his voice a low whisper. "If I can't fix the bird, I'll carve you another."

"Please don't." Isabelle's hand shook as she stared at the nest in her palm. "I like it better this way." Hollow, hopeless...heartbroken.

Preach slid his hand under hers and stared into her eyes. "Your Aunt may not be sorry for what she did, but I am. I'm sorry for the distress I've caused you. I won't bother you again."

Of course he wouldn't. No decent man would once they'd heard.

CHAPTER 4

"Wₕₐₜ do you mean she's gone? Gone where?"
Preach blinked at Lou through the crack in the
bunkhouse door before rubbing the sleep from his eyes. Her
insistent knock had broken the first three-hour stretch of
slumber he'd had in two nights. His head pounded, and it had
taken him a few moments to locate his breeches and slide them
on before he staggered to the bunkhouse door.

Lou must have just woken up, too. In the lamp's light, ratted
gray locks tumbled over the brown wool of her shawl.

"She's gone!"

"Keep your voice down. The others are finally sleeping."

"I knocked on Isabelle's door to wake her, and there was no
answer. Her bed was made up. I don't know if she slept in it or
not." She tugged the apron at her waist. "A book is missing and a
couple of dresses." Lou reached through the narrow opening
and gripped his wrist with the strength of a man. "Preach, you
have to help me. My brother would never forgive me if I...if..."
Lou covered her brow and moaned. "What have I done?"

Preach glanced over her tousled head. Thick frost coated the
trees along the clearing. It was the coldest night since the start

of the season. "She wouldn't have left last night, would she? It's a long way to Stony Creek in the dark." And much too cold if you're not accustomed to the mountain temperatures, let alone thin as a rail like Isabelle.

"I don't know. She went to bed early. She was upset at me for breaking the carving, so I let her be. I didn't look for her until this morning. Preach, she doesn't know the way to town, and the road's such a mess. She has no idea what cut-off to take. She'll never make it."

"Is she on foot?" An animal would go a long way to keeping the girl warm.

Lou glanced over her shoulder toward the corral. "I imagine so. She's never ridden. She's a city girl. That's why we need to find her before—"

"Find who?" Snoop asked rubbing his jaw. Wearing his red woolen union suit, his bristled, black hair standing on end, he'd snuck up behind Preach.

"Go back to bed." Preach turned to face Snoop so he could see Preach meant business. "The others will wake up soon and be begging for liquids. I'm going out. Lou needs my help."

When he and Lou found Isabelle, the last thing she needed was Snoop asking her questions. Lou's insult from the day before had caused her niece enough trouble.

Snoop took a step toward Preach. "I'm not likely to fall asleep now."

Snoop had slept through most of the insistent calls during the night from the men for sips of water or the use of a bedpan. He'd enjoyed a full night's sleep.

Playing nursemaid was getting old. Preach couldn't wait for the others to recover and get back to work. But it didn't matter if Preach was bone tired, he wasn't letting Snoop help in the search for Isabelle. For all Lou knew, Isabelle might have just gone to the creek to pray or whatever it was she'd been doing that day with her head tipped back, lips moving silently.

Preach's mind lingered on the image of Isabelle the first day they'd met.

"Preach?"

He looked down at Lou, seeing deep furrows lined her brow. "Don't bother trying to go back to sleep, Snoop. The men are your responsibility now that you're up. I'm leaving."

As Preach stepped outside and latched the door to speak to Lou, wisps of his breath spiraled into the crisp morning air. "Give me a few minutes, and I'll go and take a look. If she left, she probably hasn't gotten far."

"She's lost, I know she's lost."

"Not likely." Preach shrugged. "But if she wants to go, you'll have to let her." It was probably best for him and Isabelle if the girl did leave the camp. The feelings she stirred up in his gut were better left undisturbed. "She's not a prisoner, Lou."

"I promised my brother I'd take care of her until she agreed to..."

"To what?"

"My brother's business. I told him she'd be safe here. I never thought she'd take off." Lou whipped around. "Isabelle, where are you?" Her voice echoed across the camp.

Several horses turned to look, breath curling from their nostrils.

If Snoop had only suspected before, now he knew for sure there was another woman at the camp. "I'll get dressed and be with you shortly," Preach said. "Go ahead and find out if she's taken one of the horses. Give them some hay while you're at it. I'll check the creek."

"Thank you, Preach." Lou's shoulders slumped as if they had no fight left in them before she whispered, "Please find her for me."

Preach nodded before Lou turned toward the barn.

"I knew it!" Snoop sat on his bed lacing his leather boots over thick, wool socks.

"You knew nothing, ya lunkhead, now keep it down." The shine in Snoop's eyes did not bode well for trying to convince him to stay at the bunkhouse.

"Hee hee, I'll be coming into a windfall as soon as the boys are well enough to pay up. Perley set the odds at four to one. I'm not sure why you didn't wager seeing how you knew all along I was telling the truth about the curvaceous creature with the pile of sable curls walking the trail to the cookhouse."

Now the wood nymph was curvaceous? "If that's what you thought you saw, then you're mistakin'. You don't deserve the winnings."

"Don't be sore, Preach. I know what I saw. I may not have all the details precise, but I know she was beautiful."

Likely the most beautiful woman Preach had ever met. A woman versed in the scriptures, a woman who liked to care for the downtrodden. The thought buoyed his spirits.

Preach returned Snoop's insistent stare. Regardless of Preach's feelings, Lou had referred to some sort of predicament. Like Preach had been telling himself until the early hours of the morning, it was most likely the same predicament men and women have been getting into since the beginning of time. Knowledge of scripture or not, now that Preach was a pastor, he couldn't let himself be tempted by the likes of Lou's niece—as much as he would like to be.

Snoop's grin stretched across his cheeks. "I'll surmise her name was Isabelle. What does she have to do with Lou?"

"I don't have time for your questions. The girl's gone missing, probably just headed for town. I'm going to saddle up Rosie and take a look."

Snoop crossed to the stove and pulled his shirt from one of the T-shaped stands hanging from the rafters. "I'm going, too."

Preach's low whisper rumbled. "You're not. Stay here and look after the men." Preach didn't want Snoop anywhere near Isabelle.

Snoop snapped his chin Preach's direction and smirked as he fastened the last button on his checked shirt. "You look after the sorry bunch of snivelers. I'm going to find the girl. Besides, I saw her first."

Preach made a fist. Just one blow and Snoop would be lucky if he could ever smirk again. *Would You forgive me, Lord, if I hit him?*

"If you won't, Lou can look after the men." Snoop tromped to the door. "And may the best man win," he called over his shoulder and sniggered before stepping out onto the path.

Preach smashed the side of his fist against the log wall at the head of his bed. "Ouch!" he said between gritted teeth before he pressed his sore fist.

"Preach...what you doing?" The muffled words emanated from Will's bunk, his blond curls the only thing peeking from the cocoon of his wool blanket.

"Go back to sleep, Will. It's not even daybreak yet."

"I'm thirsty."

"Lou will be over shortly, let *her* know."

Preach threw on the rest of his clothes, grabbed his Mackinaw from beside the stove, and lit a lamp before stepping into the chill of the morning

There was no sign of Isabelle down at the creek or in any of the outbuildings. Preach entered the cook shack to make sure Lou hadn't been mistaken. His gaze lingered on the clothes lining the log wall in Isabelle's room, work clothes—all of them. Isabelle wasn't planning on being a cook's helper or keeping house anywhere else.

The frost crunched under Preach's boots as he crossed the yard to the makeshift barn fashioned of narrow logs, which had been stood on end and topped with a hip roof.

Lou was climbing the crude ladder to the loft.

Seven horses stomped their hooves waiting on Lou to fork

hay down into the corral as Snoop tightened the cinch on a horse he'd tied to a rail.

All animals accounted for—foolish girl.

"Which direction are you going, Snoop?"

Snoop jerked his chin up and snorted. "Any direction I please."

Preach squeezed his left hand and released it, the sting from hitting the wall a good reminder to control his temper. "There's no point in us covering the same ground."

"How do I know you won't give the girl a ride to the train station in Stony Creek? I got a lot of money riding on her showing up again. Money I need."

"For what?"

"The more I have, the more I'll get."

"You keep reassuring yourself of that." Snoop might have struck on something. If Preach gave Isabelle a ride to the station and bought her a ticket, she could go back to her family—where she belonged. It would also solve the problem of the draw he felt toward the girl. He needed an untarnished woman to settle down with.

Cheating Snoop out of his winnings when he couldn't produce the wood nymph would be icing on the cake. Preach worked to keep the elation from his voice. "Like you said, may the best man win."

Preach watched Snoop's back as he rode to the entrance of the camp where the road split into three forks. Two north forks led deep into the bush where the loggers felled their quotas of trees and the skidders piled the cut logs. The south fork, although appearing to veer away from Stony Creek, was the only fork that led to the town.

What were the chances Isabelle would recognize the road she'd traveled on in the middle of the night?

Apparently, Snoop didn't think they were high.

"Yah!" He kicked his heels into the horse's ribs as he rounded the bend of the northernmost fork.

Snoop was probably right, although Preach was figuring on Isabelle having a sense of direction. Preach thought about Isabelle's pale skin with no spots or marks to speak of—not a girl who'd spent any time outdoors. If she had taken the south fork, he could catch up with her, deliver her to the station, and be back before Snoop returned from the woods.

"You gonna keep staring off like some kind of idiot, or are you going to go and find my niece?" Lou yelled from the loft, all traces of the softened demeanor she'd shown at the bunkhouse gone.

The smell of manure stung his nostrils as he crossed the corral and snugged a finger in Rosie's halter. All the horses at the camp were bred to pull, not ride. Snoop had saddled up the youngest, probably hoping the horse's age would give him an advantage. Preach was glad Snoop hadn't taken Rosie out of spite. She might be older, but she was broke to ride. "I'll give Rosie some oats and see what I can do."

An hour and a half later and just shy of town, there was still no sign of Isabelle. There'd been no tracks on the way down, either. If she'd come this way, she'd followed the frozen road. But if she had, why hadn't Preach come across her yet?

Dawn had pushed its way into the valley about an hour before, but it hadn't warmed the air. Preach tugged the reins to draw Rosie to a halt. He rubbed his palms together and blew into his hands to warm them. It didn't help. He should have grabbed some gloves before he left.

"Where is she, Rosie?"

The horse's ear twitched.

"You'd tell me if you could, wouldn't you?" He patted the horse's withers.

If Preach was cold, Isabelle would be close to freezing. At least if Snoop had found her, she'd be on her way back to the heat of the cook stove, and Lou could care for her. More than likely she would tear a strip off the girl's hide first. There was no way Lou would let Isabelle know how anxious she'd been when Isabelle went missing.

Preach had been worrying the comment Lou had made about taking care of the girl until she agreed to do—whatever it was—for over half an hour. Could Lou have meant marry the fellow? Isn't that what most proper girls did when they'd succumbed? The thought of Isabelle marrying someone else burned in his chest.

As far as her family was concerned, she was soiled—not the kind of woman Preach needed to help him lead a flock of the Lord's people. But the closer he got to town, the less he liked the idea of finding Isabelle and putting her on the train. Maybe Snoop would find her first and take the decision out of his hands.

CHAPTER 5

*I*sabelle's teacup rattled in its saucer. Was that Preach? Of course it was Preach. Who else stood head and shoulders above everyone else, broad chested, arms wide enough to—

"Isabelle," Miss Sophie said, "are you all right?"

Isabelle inched her chair back, concealing her form behind the heavy, brocade curtains lining the window in Miss Sophie's sitting room.

Isabelle's mother would have loved the mahogany furnishings and the rich tapestry adorning the walls, although it would have been difficult to convince her she could find such refinement at the world's end. Mother had never understood why her sister-in-law preferred the "wilds" over city life.

"I'm chilled." Isabelle smiled and lifted the rim of the dainty floral cup to her lips. The Earl Grey liberally doused with milk and sugar warmed its way to her stomach.

Preach had come looking for her.

He must have left the camp before daybreak. It had taken Isabelle over four hours to walk to town after sneaking out at three o'clock in the morning. Most likely Aunt Lou had forced Preach to search for her.

It probably hadn't been fair for Isabelle to leave the camp the way she had. Surely Preach had figured out by now Isabelle was more trouble than she was worth.

But Isabelle couldn't have stayed at the camp one more day, not after she'd seen the look in Preach's eyes when he'd held her hand and apologized for causing her distress, the look of both pity and repulsion. Seeing his reaction had burned to Isabelle's core. She drew in a breath and swallowed the emotion threatening to overcome her.

Miss Sophie rose from her chair and squeezed Isabelle's forearm. "Of course you're chilly. You're as tiny as a bird. I'll stoke up the fireplace again. It will warm your limbs until the blood starts running. You had a long walk in the cold."

Tiny as a bird? Perhaps a sparrow? If only Aunt Lou hadn't destroyed Preach's beautiful gift. If only she hadn't said those dreadful words.

And if Isabelle was as tiny as a bird, what would that make Miss Sophie? The woman stood no taller than five feet. Her animated expression and quick movements belied her age. Upon meeting Isabelle an hour and a half ago, she'd exclaimed, "In all my seventy years, I've never seen someone as forlorn as you standing on the train platform."

Miss Sophie scuttled over to the tall blue-gray woodbin against the far wall and plucked two lengths of wood from the box before opening the door on the Franklin stove. A blast of hot air filled the room.

Isabelle closed her eyes as the heat enveloped her, encouraging it to chase away the chill of both body and soul.

Miss Sophie cleared her throat. Twisting a gray curl that had escaped her chignon, she said, "If you don't mind me asking, is it Preach you're running from?"

Isabelle's gaze flicked to the view of main street outside the window—no sign of him. "Umm, no, well—"

"I'd be disappointed to hear it was. We've seen such a change in him."

"We?" Miss Sophie had mentioned she lived alone as her husband had died of a heart attack ten years earlier.

"The church. Preach has been coming down the mountain on Sundays to share the word with us ever since Mr. Miller, our former pastor, broke his hip falling off his horse."

"He's an actual pastor?" Preach had left that part out when he'd written about how he loved sharing the gospel with the men at the camp and the folks of Stony Creek. No wonder he was disappointed with her.

"He doesn't have any formal training, and we don't pay him. He told us he makes enough money logging. But I'll tell you, that young man shares with a conviction I haven't heard in a long time. It's a real change from what he used to do when he came to town."

Isabelle raised an eyebrow.

Miss Sophie adjusted the lace jabot of her burgundy day-dress before continuing. "Living here, in the center of Main Street, not much escapes my notice. One of the reasons I darted over to tell you the train wouldn't be arriving until tomorrow."

"I'm so grateful you did." If Sophie hadn't noticed Isabelle reading the schedule on the train station door and invited her over to warm up, Preach would have found her by now, and she would be headed up the mountain—straight back to Aunt Lou.

"Preach and some of the other boys from Pollitt's Lumber would come into town the first Saturday of the month. They caused quite a stir with their rough looks and crude ways. By late evening, they'd be swaying down Main Street calling out insults to each other and roughhousing. They often broke shop windows or damaged wagons with their antics." Miss Sophie tidied the stack of books resting on parlor table at her elbow.

"Those of us who live in Stony Creek learned to stay home on those Saturdays. Milton, he owns the Belt Buckle Saloon, is the only one of us who was thankful for the lumberjacks' arrival. He makes more money on Saturday nights than on all the others put together."

It was hard to imagine Preach, gentle and protective as he was, intoxicated and obnoxious. "So Preach doesn't come to town on Saturdays anymore?"

"He still comes with the others, only now he acts as a chaperone. If the boys get too unruly and start breaking up people's property, he sends them back up the mountain or finds them a place to sleep the drink off. If he can convince one or two, he brings them to church the next morning. The congregation is getting used to snores and snorts from the back pews where Preach deposits them before he gets up to give his sermon."

The scenario Miss Sophie portrayed would not happen back home at Grace Church. Rough sorts were not allowed through the imposing white doors of her Seattle neighborhood church. If offenders managed to sneak in, the ushers would promptly march them back out. It was a good thing the ushers couldn't read the thoughts of those sitting in the pews during a Sunday morning service, or they might have had to escort the entire congregation onto the church lawn. "I'm surprised the church members put up with it."

"Granted, it has taken some of them a while to get used to it." A soft giggle escaped Miss Sophie's lips, she covered her mouth with gnarled fingers and hunched her shoulders.

Isabelle couldn't resist joining Miss Sophie, and the two of them giggled until they laughed.

It had been so long since Isabelle had found anything amusing, let alone funny, she laughed until she clutched her stomach to keep it from paining. "Miss Sophie, stop, please. All this laughter is making my stomach hurt."

Miss Sophie's eyes sparkled with mischief as she reached

across and patted Isabelle's hand. "A merry heart doeth good like a medicine, young lady, and you look like you could use a spoonful. I know it's early for lunch, but I'm going to fix you a sandwich. You stay here by the fire."

Isabelle placed her tea on the side table, plucked her gloves from her lap, and stood. "Please don't go to any more trouble—"

"Sit down, dear." Miss Sophie swatted the air as she beelined toward the kitchen. "It's no trouble. I enjoy the company."

Isabelle returned her gloves to her lap and rolled her shoulders back. The heat from the fire had finally wormed its way into her bones, and she'd stopped shivering. It was foolish not to have worn extra layers for warmth when she'd set out from the camp with only a few belongings in her carpet bag and a lantern to guide her way down the treacherous road. If she'd been thinking, she could have borrowed Aunt Lou's overcoat, oversized as it was, and left word it was at the station before boarding the train for home.

Surely Isabelle would be welcomed home by now. She'd suffered two weeks at the camp. It was long enough for Father to see reason, or perhaps long enough for Mother to convince him of such.

On the final morning before leaving for the camp, Father had railed about her ungratefulness and shoved papers around his desk while Mother had leaned against his office door frame and cried. It was the last time he'd presented the ultimatum. "You *will* do as I say, young lady," he'd shouted, cheeks afire, spittle flying.

When Isabelle had slowly shaken her head, Mother had gasped and Father had brought his fist down on his desk, rattling the room. "We'll see about that." He'd pushed past Mother and left the office. That very evening, he'd driven Isabelle to the logging camp.

Perhaps if she wrote and asked Mother for her permission to

come home and Isabelle didn't just show up at the door, it would help Father accept her arrival.

"Here you are." Miss Sophie placed a porcelain luncheon plate on the table holding a crustless egg salad sandwich and two beet pickles. "I imagine you'll be heading back up to the camp with Preach. Do you think you'll come back tomorrow to take the train? I'm not sure why they let you come down today in the first place, all that way without an escort."

Isabelle took another bite of the sandwich and a sip of tea to keep the egg from lodging in her throat. She'd only told Miss Sophie she meant to take the train home and not that no one knew she was leaving, or arriving for that matter. "I should let my parents know I'll be arriving tomorrow. Could I use your telephone?"

"Oh, child, there are no telephones in town yet, but we are lucky enough to have a telegraph office."

A telegram would suffice. A messenger could have the note to her parents' door within a quarter hour of Isabelle sending it, and if Mother was at home, Isabelle could receive a reply within the same hour. If the answer was yes, she could take a room in town until the morrow and hope Preach or Aunt Lou didn't find Isabelle before she could board the train.

"Your parents let you travel alone? A girl your age?"

What could happen that hadn't already happened? But her parents didn't know about that. "I'm sure they'd much rather I had a companion, but that is not possible. I'll mention to the porter that I'm travelling alone. He'll see to it I'm not bothered by any strange men who might want to steal a kiss in a tunnel."

"Dear me." Sophie fiddled with her lace jabot once more. "Is that what this world has come to?"

"I didn't mean to alarm you. It's most likely just a myth. Most train travel has proven safe for women traveling alone." Isabelle smiled, willing Miss Sophie to believe her.

47

"I'll walk you over to the telegraph office. Ellis, my friend Millicent's son, runs it and the post office, too."

"I don't want to be any more bother," Isabelle said. "You've warmed me up and given me food. I really should be on my way." Whatever way that might be after Isabelle heard from Mother.

"Nonsense. I must post the letter I wrote to my sister yesterday. Finish up while I fetch my coat."

Isabelle forked the beet pickles into her mouth. Their tangy sweetness bit her tongue before slipping down her throat. Miss Sophie's pickles rivaled Aunt Lou's for flavor, but with any luck, that truth wouldn't be something Isabelle would have the opportunity to share with her aunt.

A brisk walk down Main Street brought them to a narrow white clapboard structure with a large picture window.

"Good morning, Miss Sophie." A slender young man wearing a crisp white shirt, a tie, and a wool vest called out from his seat at a wide table behind the counter running the length of the building. Above his head, the clock ticked to a quarter past nine.

The hour was early. Isabelle's mother would be at home.

As they approached the scuffed counter, Ellis glanced at Isabelle, straightened his spine, and tugged the two points of his vest before stepping to the counter. "Is this young lady a relative? I hadn't heard you—"

"Not a relative, a friend." Out of his sight, Miss Sophie clutched Isabelle's fingers and squeezed.

"But..." Ellis drew his heavy brows together and tilted his head. "When did she arrive?"

Laughter bubbled from Miss Sophie's throat. "If there's anyone who knows more about what goes on in this town than I do, it would be you, Ellis. This is my friend, Miss Isabelle Franklin. Isabelle, Mr. Ellis Wherry."

Isabelle gave a small curtsy. "It's so nice to meet you, Mr. Wherry. I was hoping I could send a telegram, please."

"Oh, indeed." Ellis shuffled several papers on his desk before he placed a telegram form and a fountain pen on the counter in front of her.

Isabelle stared at the bold Western Union letters across the top of the form until they blurred on the page. What should she say? How should she ask? Isabelle could not fulfill Father's wishes, yet she desperately wanted—no needed—to go home.

Ellis cleared his throat. "The cost is twenty-five cents, ten words or less."

"I—I just need a few moments, if you don't mind."

Lifting both palms outward, Ellis stepped back from the counter. "Take all the time you need. There's a bench in the corner."

"I'll leave you to your telegram and go pick up the meat I ordered yesterday at the butcher's." Miss Sophie placed her letter on the smooth wood of the counter. "Ellis, if you would post this to my sister. Isabelle, come back to the house when you're finished. I'll keep the fire stoked."

"Thank you," Isabelle whispered as the door creaked open behind her.

"So you're alive. Good to know."

Preach. Her stomach lurched. Of course, it had only been a matter of time until he found her. Isabelle swiped at her eyes and rounded to face him.

"Good morning, Miss Sophie." Preach nodded to her companion.

"Good morning, Preach." Miss Sophie touched Isabelle's coat sleeve. "I'll be about my errands now, Isabelle, I'll see you back at the house when you're finished."

As Miss Sophie left the post office, Isabelle stared at the floor. Where should she begin? It wasn't fair to make Aunt Lou worry, that was true. Isabelle was sorry she'd left the camp the way she had. That wasn't true—not after the way Preach had looked at her when Aunt Lou had said what she'd said.

As she was packing up, Isabelle had rolled the nest Preach had given her inside a spare skirt before stuffing it into her carpet bag, the carpet bag which now sat on the floor inside Miss Sophie's front door. The nest would serve as a reminder of the kind man. A man she had grown to care for but would have to try and forget.

"I'm going home."

"Your aunt's beside herself."

Isabelle glanced up. Preach's expression was difficult to read. Were his brows wrinkled because he was worried or because he was angry? "I'm sorry, I shouldn't have left without leaving a note."

"You shouldn't have left. Someone could have brought you to town tomorrow, when the train comes through. It was dangerous, leaving the way you did."

She set her jaw. "If I'd asked, Aunt Lou wouldn't have let me leave."

"If you'd asked *me*, I would have brought you to town. Like I told Lou, you're not a prisoner." Preach reached out and took her elbow. The warmth of his fingers pulsed through her coat and up her arm.

Isabelle wasn't in visible chains, but if Father had his way, she might as well be.

Ellis cleared his throat, and Preach dropped his fingers from Isabelle's elbow.

"Are you ready to send your telegram?" Ellis asked.

Preach blinked.

"I thought I should let my parents know I'd be arriving. I'm not sure..." Isabelle wasn't sure of anything anymore.

"Not sure of what?" His gaze searched hers.

It still carried the look—the look of near disdain it had taken on the moment Aunt Lou had voiced those ugly words the night before. A lump formed in Isabelle's throat, and she dropped her voice to a whisper. "If they'll let me come home."

"Go ahead and send your telegram," Preach said. "We'll have coffee while you're waiting for a reply."

Isabelle stepped to the counter. Ten words would be more than enough.

Mrs. Emily Franklin
4589 Northlake Way
Seattle, Washington

Please, may I come home?

Isabelle

Ellis took the form and a quarter. As Isabelle and Preach left the post office, the telegraph operator tap tapped the message to her mother.

CHAPTER 6

$\mathcal{A}$ brass shop bell *brrringed* as Preach opened the door and motioned for Isabelle to precede him into the Blue Jay Eating House. After swiping the hat from his head and looking over his shoulder, he followed her. The entrance was steps from the alley, a small alcove on the side of a low brick building behind the druggist's shop. The arrangement kept the guardians of the town's business from seeing exactly who was dining with whom.

Although he frequented May's place on weekends, Preach had never needed the secrecy before. The discreet entrance would give Isabelle some privacy and prevent an assault by members of the congregation who were convinced Preach would make a fine husband for their daughters. The mothers had been relentless since his return to the camp and his offer to preach at Stony Creek Chapel. It appeared the congregants had more faith in Preach's ability to walk the narrow path than he did.

Isabelle's proximity didn't help his resolve either. Her flaw-less skin and pretty brown eyes enticed more than his frequent glances. Although she deserved a better comparison, Isabelle reminded Preach of an actress he'd watched perform in a musical comedy back home. They called her La Favorita, a woman it was best to forget.

Preach glanced at Isabelle. Her face was empty of the little color it usually owned. She was probably famished from her long hike into Stony Creek, foolish woman. Even if it was necessary for her to leave, there was no need for her to walk the whole way.

"Well, look who's in town on a weekday morning." May's voice rang out from behind the luncheon counter, where she filled a white mug from the spigot of an oversized nickel coffee urn.

Three of the men at the counter turned and met Preach's gaze before taking in Isabelle from head to toe. With eyebrows raised, they returned to their food.

Preach probably should have taken her to Ming's Cafe on Main, busy bodies or not. "We'll have two coffees, May," he said before tugging a scuffed bentwood chair back from one of the empty tables. He nodded, inviting Isabelle to sit.

The girl hadn't said a word since she'd sent the telegram. "You all right?" He took the chair opposite.

"I'm tired. The walk into town was a long one."

"Why didn't you use one of the horses?"

She widened her eyes into almost a glare. "Ha. I wanted to arrive in one piece. I've only ridden on miniature ponies at the fair when I was a young girl."

"How'd you get by, not learning to ride?"

"We've always lived in the city. As long as I can remember, we owned a carriage and hired a driver. My father wanted to rise above the humble life he had as a child."

Not a country girl. He already knew that.

"You must be famished," he said. "Could I buy you an early lunch? I'm sure May can rustle something up. She won't see a crowd for another two hours." Preach thrust his chin at

Isabelle. "You need to start putting some meat on those bones."

Isabelle dropped her gaze to the table before fiddling with a teaspoon next to the plain white sugar bowl.

What a fool thing to say. "Sorry, I shouldn't have commented—"

"On what? Something that's painfully obvious. I've been unwell." The words were barely above a murmur. "For six months. That's why my father sent me here. That and..." Isabelle shrugged.

Aunt Lou had made sure Preach guessed the other reason too. But sending your daughter off to a logging camp to be worked off her feet so she could recuperate? A camp full of men desperate for the company of woman? The plan didn't make her father sound like a wise man.

Preach reached out and covered the hand fidgeting with the spoon. Her tapered fingers were soft and surprisingly warm as they stilled beneath his.

"Here you go, two coffees."

Preach withdrew his hand from Isabelle's as May plunked the cups between them. A splash of liquid from Preach's mug landed on the tablecloth, and a brown stain bloomed from the base of his mug, marring the bleached whiteness. At twice his age, May wasn't much to look at with her heavy brows and large features, but she was a stickler for cleanliness. Preach searched May's face, eyes dark as a storm cloud. What was her problem?

"You folks care for menus? Soup won't be ready until noon. Most everything else is available."

"Please."

May pulled two menus from under her muscular arm, laid them on the table, and spoke as she walked away. "Let me know when you're ready."

Isabelle cleared her throat as Preach passed her a menu. "I don't think she likes me."

So May's attitude *was* obvious. "Does she know you? I didn't think you'd ever left the camp until today."

"I've never met her before."

"Then she can't know if she likes you or not."

As Isabelle dipped her head to study her menu, the corners of her mouth turned up in a small smile, the first one he'd seen since he'd given her the carving the night before. If only he could make the smile last.

Preach glanced at the menu. Skipping breakfast meant he was hungrier than usual—and that was saying something. According to Lou, the twenty-one men at the camp ate more than three times what the average man consumed. Isabelle probably had some idea, helping Lou and all, but she'd never watched the men tuck into the food before. It was something to behold, not a word said between them as they chowed down on mountains of foodstuffs. He'd have to cut back or he would scare the poor girl, and it looked as if she'd been scared enough.

"Have you decided on something?" he asked.

"I'm hungrier than usual. I'll have two poached eggs and toast, please."

"And?"

Isabelle cocked her head. "And the coffee? Miss Sophie made me a sandwich not long ago."

Only two poached eggs on toast? It wasn't even an appetizer. That would explain the size of the girl. Preach, on his own, could eat a dozen eggs in one breakfast, and that was before he moved onto the ham and beans. He stared at the menu. It was looking like he would be hungry a while longer. "May, we're ready."

Twenty minutes later, Isabelle laid her fork and knife diagonally across her plate before thanking him for the breakfast. Egg yolk pooled next to the half slice of brown toast on her plate.

Preach resisted the urge to drag her toast through the yolk and stuff it into his mouth in one bite. The double order of a frizzled beef omelet and a side of beans hadn't touched the growl in his stomach.

The door opened, and a cool breeze swept into the room. Phyllis Thorebourne, wife of the owner at Thorebourne Timber Company, stepped inside. Preach glanced at May, who avoided his gaze as she wiped the counter. Had May sent word he was in Stony Creek? Probably not. May and Phyllis were unlikely cohorts.

With a tower of feathers and ribbons bobbing on her straw hat, Phyllis tromped across the patterned oilcloth floor to their table. "Good morning, Preach," she said, and crossed her arms over her imposing bosom. "Who might this young lady be?"

Phyllis was the church pianist and the most fervent champion for a daughter's hopes in landing Preach as a future husband. It wasn't the girl's fault he didn't find her near six feet of height and sculpted features appealing. He simply preferred women who looked less capable. Women with pale skin, sparkling eyes, brown hair down to their—who was he fooling? Women like Isabelle, future wife or not.

Preach cleared his throat. "Mrs. Thorebourne, how nice to see you. Meeting someone for coffee?" He glanced at May, still scrubbing at the same spot at the counter. It must be quite the stain.

"Just stepping in to see my sister." Phyllis nodded, and the ribbons and feathers bobbed as though agreeing with her.

"May's your sister?" So May *had* sent word. Now, knowing the truth, he could see the resemblance between the two women. May was a stronger, thinner version of Phyllis. Josephine, Phyllis's daughter, had been fashioned from a different mold altogether.

"May's not much for baking," Phyllis said, "so I supply the desserts for the house. Who's your friend?" Tossing her chin, the feathers and ribbons went at it again.

"I'm—"

"So you're the one who makes those delicious apple dumplings with the hard sauce?" *Sorry, Isabelle.* But it was none of Phyllis's business who Isabelle was, she was planning to leave town anyway. "I think I might have one. It's never too early for an apple dumpling. May," he called across the room, "two orders of apple dumplings with hard sauce please."

May ducked behind the narrow canvas curtain dividing the dining room from the kitchen.

Isabelle said, "I don't think—"

"'Shaw, you'll love 'em. I promise." Ignoring Isabelle's wide eyes, he focused on the woman standing beside them. "It's good to see you, Mrs. Thorebourne. We won't hold you up. You have a good day, now." Preach slurped at his coffee, hoping Phyllis would take the hint.

Phyllis planted her feet and stretched a beefy hand toward Isabelle.

Apparently the woman wasn't going to give up easily.

"Phyllis Thorebourne. So nice to meet you."

Isabelle's gaze flicked to Preach's before she cautiously extended her hand toward Phyllis's. "Nice to meet you, I'm Isabelle Franklin."

All right, Phyllis. You have her name, now move along.

Phyllis leaned in, bringing her eyes level with Isabelle's. "And how do the two of you know each other?"

"I'm assistant cook at Pollitt's logging camp."

Phyllis dropped Isabelle's right hand while glancing at her left one. "Assistant cook? You're married?"

"N–no."

"You're not? Lou said Joe was particular about not having unmarried women at the camp. Not that my Josephine needs a position, but she's a wonderful cook."

Here Phyllis went.

"She helps me cook for her brothers. She's got four."

He sat back, waiting for the same words she always spoke next. *They're big boys, used to hard work, big appetites.*

Phyllis preened a little. "They're big boys, used to hard work, big appetites."

Just as he'd expected. Truth was, it didn't matter to Preach how well, or how much, Josephine could cook. If courting was only about satisfying his stomach, Preach might as well marry Lou.

"I guess they took me on because I'm her niece."

"Her niece?" Phyllis stepped back and stared at Isabelle as though comparing her to Lou.

There was no comparison. "May," Preach called, "are you coming with those dumplings? We'll have another coffee, too. Phyllis, it's been nice talking—"

"So, you're Lou's niece? The woman doesn't admit to having any family, period, yet here you are. It doesn't change the fact Joe doesn't want eligible woman at the camp. He said it gets the men too worked up."

Joe was right. Isabelle had caused all kinds of excitement, and most of the men didn't even know if she was real or not. The poor girl looked like she wanted to crawl under the table to escape Phyllis's scrutiny.

May finally entered the dining room with their desserts.

Phyllis didn't need to know Joe had no idea Isabelle was at the camp either. "I guess he changed his mind," Preach said. "Excuse us. We'd like to enjoy our dumplings while they're hot."

May removed their used dishes and served the dumplings.

Steam rose from a large pastry-covered apple at the center of each plate. Brandy sauce coated the top and sides of each dumpling and pooled generously around the base. A dollop of hard sauce, his favorite part, melted into the brandy sauce. His mouth watered.

Isabelle picked up her fork. "These look delicious. Thank you."

May retreated behind the counter, but Phyllis made no move to let them eat without her company.

"Please excuse us, Mrs. Thorebourne," he said, hoping she'd note the sternness in his voice.

"I'd like to say, perhaps we'll meet again but judging by the sight of you, I don't think you'll last long." Phyllis arched one eyebrow as though daring Preach to argue with her.

Isabelle stilled in bringing the steaming bite of apple and pastry to her lips.

Preach took in her dropped chin and the moisture collecting at the corner of her eyes. How could Isabelle help it if she'd been sick? "Look here, that wasn't a kind thing to say. Why don't you apologize?" In less than twenty-four hours, Preach had asked two women to say they were sorry to Isabelle. She appeared to invite more torment than she deserved. If only he could reach over and wipe the tears from her eyes.

Phyllis crossed her arms. "I'm not apologizing. Anyone with eyes can see the truth of it. The girl won't last long working up the mountain with Lou."

"Excuse us, Phyllis, we *mean* to eat our dumplings while they're hot."

Phyllis finally heard reason and marched behind the counter with May. The two of them disappeared into the kitchen, whispering. Phyllis most likely telling May who the interloper was. It didn't matter how much finagling the two women did, Preach wasn't interested in Josephine.

"I'm sorry she was rude, even if Phyllis isn't. The woman thinks she has everything figured out."

Isabelle stared at her plate, the bite of dessert cooling on her fork. "It's understandable. I shouldn't have agreed to come here with you. It gives people the wrong notion."

Was she referring to the notion that seeing her beautiful smile made his heart flop over in his chest? It wouldn't be the wrong notion at all. "I'm not sure—"

"My father shouldn't have sent me to the camp. I'm not much use. I'm sorry you were seen with me."

"What are you talking about?"

"Here, in town, you know, with my past."

He couldn't take it, his throat pained at the sight of her desolate face. "Look." Preach took Isabelle's hand. Her soft fingers felt like they belonged in his. Perhaps he'd judged her too soon. "I don't know your past. Your aunt alluded to one, but I'd like to hear the story from you. We all have pasts, stuff we'd like to forget." Preach had a lot of stuff he'd like to forget about before he was saved.

Isabelle drew her hand from under his. "I'm sorry. The dumpling looks delicious, but I'm not hungry any more. If you'll excuse me, I'm going to walk back to the post office and see if I've received a reply yet."

His chair scraped on the floor as Preach pushed back from the table and rose.

Isabelle's gaze pleaded with his and she held up her palm. "Please, stay and eat. I'd like to go alone. I'll wait at the post office until I have word from my mother. If you wouldn't mind stopping by Miss Sophie's in an hour or so, I should know by then if I'll be leaving on the train tomorrow. If not, I guess I'll go back to the camp." She plucked her kid gloves from her lap, pulled them on, and tugged on the cuffs before flashing him a quick smile. After thanking him for the breakfast, she left the eating house.

Preach picked up his fork and speared the dumpling off Isabelle's plate. Brandy sauce trailed in blotches across the table and joined the coffee in staining May's tablecloth. It served her right for all her meddling. In two bites, Isabelle's dumpling disappeared. Bland and sticky, it was nothing like he remembered. He dropped his fork beside his own dumpling. For the first time since he was a young'un eating Brussels sprouts, he would be leaving food on his plate.

CHAPTER 7

*I*sabelle checked the clock ticking out time on the wall above Ellis's head. Ten thirty, she'd been sitting on the bench in the corner for over half an hour. A quiet day, according to Ellis, as the mail only arrived with the train on Tuesdays and Fridays. Three times her stomach tightened its knot at the tapping of the telegraph receiver. Each time, Ellis had looked across the room and shaken his head. What was keeping Mother's reply?

Thank goodness Ellis had given up trying to engage Isabelle in conversation and had resorted to organizing his desk. He shuffled through disorderly piles of paper, occasionally trotting over to a filing cabinet with a map of the country stretched above it and depositing a paper or two in one of the drawers.

Isabelle covered her stomach and shifted on the bench. It was a good thing she hadn't eaten May's apple dumpling. It had looked delicious, but she was having a hard enough time keeping the eggs and toast down.

Preach was probably having second thoughts about buying Isabelle breakfast at the Blue Jay. Phyllis was a lot like Stella back home. Most likely, Phyllis wouldn't stop digging until she learned the truth about why Isabelle was hidden away on Cougar Ridge Mountain with her aunt. If Phyllis had set her sights on Preach as a son in law, true or not, in Phyllis's mind, Isabelle was an impediment to her daughter's happiness.

Phyllis was right about one thing though, anyone could tell Isabelle wasn't cut out to be a logging camp cook assistant, and that would prove to anyone who thought about it someone was trying to keep her out of sight. And what reason would any father have to keep his daughter out of sight other than he didn't want her to bring ruin on his family? If Phyllis ferreted out the information, Aunt Lou's decision to allow Isabelle to join her at the camp would also cost Aunt Lou her reputation.

Preach, as well. He should have stayed clear of Isabelle. What pastor needed the company of a pathetic soul like her?

Tap tap tap. Once again, the telegraph receiver sprung to life beside Ellis's desk. He cocked his ear and listened to the sounds as they clipped out a steady beat. His gaze traveled to Isabelle's before he rose to tear the tape from the machine.

"Is the message for me?"

Ellis pulled a slip of paper from the pigeon hole behind the receiver. "Yes, I'll have your copy ready in a moment."

Finally! Isabelle dashed across the floor, ducked behind the counter, and stood next to Ellis to peer over his shoulder as he transcribed the message.

"Look here," he said, the skin around his collar turning a deep red. "Customers are supposed to wait in front of the counter. I'll be with you shortly."

Isabelle looked at the narrow paper tape lined with meaningless ink dots and lines Ellis had placed on the desk.

"Would you please just tell me what it says?"

"If you will kindly wait in front of the counter, I'll have your copy to you shortly."

Ellis was stalling. The news wasn't what Isabelle wanted to hear—his frown implied it.

Surely, Isabelle's father would allow her to return home. Over the last two weeks, Aunt Lou had made certain Isabelle no longer languished in bed. There had to be a better solution than hiding her away in Aunt Lou's care—a solution that required work that Isabelle was more suited to, and one that did not require seeing the disappointed look in Preach's eyes.

It had been a mistake not to ask for Aunt Lou's help in convincing Father she should come home. Aunt Lou could have let her parents know how much better Isabelle was doing and that it was time to let her rejoin the family.

If, as Father thought, Isabelle's chances of a good marriage were over, perhaps she could become a governess or a teacher. Father would never allow it in Seattle, but Isabelle could go anywhere—anywhere Preach wasn't.

Ellis laid the telegram on the counter.

Isabelle stared at the words scrawled on the paper, a blot of ink accenting the *i* in Franklin.

Isabelle Franklin

You may only return home when you have accepted the offer of marriage from Daniel.

Your father

Isabelle shook as she lifted the paper and returned to the bench in the corner. Father couldn't possibly mean it. Although it was why he'd sent her to the camp in the first place, Isabelle had made it clear she would never marry Daniel. It didn't matter where Father sent her. Did he think he could keep Isabelle at the camp forever? She crumpled the telegram slip and tossed it to the floor before twisting it under her boot.

There was no point in a reply. Under no circumstances would Isabelle be marrying Daniel P. Talbot.

The memory of the warm spring day, full of promise, and the last time she'd seen Daniel still caused Isabelle's heart to pound, her throat to squeeze its breaths, and heat to flash through her entire body.

"*D*aniel!" *Isabelle lifted Daniel's white glove from the silk layers covering her upper thigh as the carriage clattered over the ruts of Lakeside Drive.*

His breath smelled of alcohol, and the liquor made him bold. Getting into the carriage, when he'd arrived alone, had not been wise on Isabelle's part.

"I love that about you, my little cherub," he said, pinching the flesh of her right cheek.

Isabelle pulled away and massaged the sting. Hopefully the mark would be gone by the time they arrived at the Allens'.

Daniel said he loved her almost every time they were together, though it was never clear why. "What do you love about me, Daniel?" Perhaps he was attracted to her cheerful disposition or her unwavering faith.

"Your feigned reluctance, my dear."

Isabelle slid farther away on the bench and turned to face him. Was the man serious?

A smirk played at the corners of his lips.

"Feigned? My reluctance is not feigned. What has gotten into you? How much did you imbibe before arriving at my home?"

Daniel pulled a sterling silver flask from the inside pocket of his black coat. "Not nearly enough." He flipped the lid back with his thumb. Holding the flask aloft, he poured a long gulp of the amber liquid. "Would you care for some?" He tipped the flask toward her.

"No, Daniel, I would not. Nor should you have any more."

Daniel scooted closer, crushing Isabelle against the smooth wood of the carriage wall. "Come now. You can tell me what you want."

"You're wrinkling my dress. I'll arrive at the ball a complete fright." Slipping her elbow between them, she wedged Daniel away and smoothed the light gray silk of her skirt.

What had gotten into him? Until tonight, he had always acted the gentleman. As the nephew of her father's business partner and the man most likely to assume the management of Franklin, Talbot, and Sons Accountants, both families had encouraged the courtship.

Daniel lifted the flask to his lips once more and swallowed. "Empty." He sneered. "That will be rectified when we arrive at this ridiculous ball."

"Ridiculous ball? Why did you ask me to attend if it's so ridiculous?"

Daniel snorted. "It's what I'm expected to do, isn't it? Trot the little darling around to the events of the season until we enter into wedded bliss." Daniel mimicked holding a bouquet of flowers and batted his eyelashes like a young girl.

He had gone too far in his jesting. Isabelle twisted on the bench and stared out the window. She'd been so thrilled when Daniel had invited her to the Allen family's May ball. Cornelius Talbot, Daniel's uncle and a former college roommate of Louis Allen, owned a standing invite to the most notable private ball of the spring season. Isabelle's family had never received an invitation.

Isabelle's mother, as thrilled as Isabelle herself about the invitation, had helped her pick a dress design. Their seamstress, Charlotte, had not disappointed them when she'd sewn an amazing creation of soft gray silk with yellow scalloped tulle sleeves. Large yellow embroidered butterflies trailed down the skirt and around the hem. Isabelle and her mother had fashioned the tea-colored roses stitched along the neckline and over one shoulder. Even Father had remarked on how well the color of the dress suited Isabelle's complexion.

Daniel had not said a single word about Isabelle's dress or the care she'd taken in braiding her hair when she had strolled into the vestibule that evening to find him conversing with Father and tapping one black oxford against the gleaming floor. The departure from her home had been hurried, bordering on rude, as he'd simply tossed her cloak over his arm and escorted her out the door. Judging by his current behavior, Isabelle should not have left with him.

Isabelle's mother would be horrified to hear how Daniel acted under the influence of strong spirits.

Etiquette required all interactions within Daniel and Isabelle's courtship to be chaperoned. Even so, without her parents' knowledge, she and Daniel had met alone on two occasions after he had persuaded her it would allow them to get to know one another better.

Isabelle had agreed that the scrutiny of every conversation during their outings and visits in the parlor had grown irksome. When Daniel had suggested the unescorted ride to the dance a few days before, Isabelle hadn't argued. In fact, the suggestion had brought a pleasant tingle to her stomach. The thrill of their clandestine journey was now gone. "My parents will be upset when they discover you've taken me out alone."

Daniel pinched the brim of his gray hat. How had she ever taken his natty clothes and extensive grooming as anything other than conceit?

Daniel huffed. "As for the word taken, it's hardly fair, my dear. You were happy enough to step into the carriage. But don't worry, there's no need for them to know. I've arranged for Peter and his sister to deliver Kittie to the ball. He's taken a shine to her, you know."

Dear, sweet Kittie deserved someone as kind as Peter. Kittie wouldn't have compromised herself—like Isabelle had.

"Kittie thinks your father is delivering you to the ball, as that's what I told Peter."

Why had Daniel planned so extensively to get Isabelle alone in the carriage? It was only a ten-minute ride to the Allens' home in the Central District.

"I'm not feeling well, Daniel. Would you please return me to my home? I won't be bothered at all if you go on to the dance. I'm sure

you'll find several young ladies willing to add you to their card." More than several, Daniel's arrival last October to work at Father's company had caused excitement in mothers across the city.

At times, Isabelle had enjoyed the green in the other girls' eyes as Daniel escorted her to the dance floor. His golden brown hair, swept back from a widow's peak, fell in waves to his shoulders. When he'd gazed at her, twirling around the floor, his dark eyes had carried intelligence and compassion. His full lips, with their adorable pucker in the center, had promised Isabelle passion.

That Daniel was nothing like the man he was behaving like today. Isabelle didn't want to get to know this Daniel.

"Sick or not, I wouldn't want you to give up so easily. I'm sure if Miles takes us on a jaunt out in the country, you'll feel much better for the fresh air."

"What fresh air?" Daniel had locked the carriage up tight in spite of the mild spring weather.

He pressed himself against her as he leaned over to open the window and signal the driver to detour further along the lakeside. Doing so, he sent her chiffon hat tumbling from her head.

Isabelle clutched the hat in her lap to keep it from falling to the carriage floor. "I don't want to go, take me home. You can give the Allens my regrets."

Daniel closed the window before bracing his arm across her bodice. Leaning in, he placed a kiss on her neck at the base of her ear.

Isabelle pressed her shoulders into the corner. The stink of Daniel's breath rolled her stomach. He'd never been so rough. "Daniel! What are you doing? Take me home right now or I'll call for your driver!"

He bent his head to her neck once more and laughed against her skin. The vibration slunk down her spine.

"Orin's my man. He won't hear you, he never does."

∿

sabelle's legs were wooden pegs. Even though her arm was looped through Daniel's, she still faltered on the top step leading to the wraparound porch of the Allens' sprawling two-story home. Fairy lights nestled on the window ledges cast a glow on their passage to the front door.

As they approached the hosts, Daniel patted Isabelle's grip on his sleeve and smiled widely enough to expose both upper and lower teeth —predator's teeth.

Nausea rolled up from the throbbing in Isabelle's stomach. She swallowed the urge to heave. Why had Daniel insisted on attending the ball after what had just happened?

"Mr. and Mrs. Allen, good evening." Daniel tipped his head.

There was nothing good about this evening. Pain coursed down Isabelle's thighs as Daniel nudged her into the home.

Kittie started across the oak paneled foyer toward them, waving, Peter in her wake.

Another heave. Isabelle couldn't face Kittie, not now. Her best friend since their governesses let them play in the park together as young girls, Kittie wouldn't understand. She wouldn't understand why Isabelle had gotten in the coach alone with Daniel. And Isabelle would never tell her, never tell a soul, what had occurred in the carriage.

Kittie didn't like Daniel. She had put up with him for Isabelle's sake, but more than once she'd warned Isabelle that he wasn't what he pretended to be—a gentleman. She'd pointed out the lingering gaze on another woman's face, the prolonged holding of a mother's hand, and the rumors of impropriety that had surfaced from his former hometown.

Isabelle had ignored all of Kittie's warnings and, on several occasions, had accused her of being jealous.

"I'm sorry, Mrs. Allen." Isabelle yanked in a breath. "I'm not feeling well. Would you please direct me to the toilet?"

Mr. Allen blinked back his surprise.

"Yes," Mrs. Allen turned toward the hall. "Come with me."

Kittie's eyes widened as Isabelle let Mrs. Allen whisk her away from the congested foyer.

"In here." Mrs. Allen opened a paneled door before prompting Isabelle to enter the tiled bath by pressing the center of her back. "Do you need anything?" she asked, searching Isabelle's face before lifting a fine eyebrow.

Yes, Isabelle needed something. She needed to go home, climb in her bed, and pretend the evening never happened.

CHAPTER 8

$\mathcal{P}$ reach doffed his cap when he entered the post office and met Ellis's gaze. Ellis shrugged and jerked his head toward the corner of the room. Isabelle was seated on a bench staring at a wrinkled telegram slip.

Her face bore no smile, and she looked as if she'd been run over by a carriage. The telegram had not brought good news. Preach crossed the floor, but Isabelle did not look up.

"Miss Franklin."

She continued to stare at the paper now quaking in her hands. When Preach sat on the bench next to her, she flinched.

After scooting several inches away, he spoke in a soft voice. "I didn't mean to startle you. When I didn't find you at Miss Sophie's, I thought you might still be here. Are you all right?"

Isabelle exhaled. "I don't suppose I am all right. Here's my father's response to my request." She passed him the telegram.

Preach read the short message. His heart twisted when he realized he'd been right. Her father demanded the couple be married. Who was this Daniel? "You're to be married?" His voice cracked as he said the words. Isabelle's gaze drew to his.

"*No. I'm not.*"

The vehemence in her voice surprised him. Isabelle's dark eyes dared him not to believe her.

"Your father wants you to marry Daniel, but you don't want to?"

"My father wants me to marry Daniel, my mother would let me choose my own destiny. I would like to become a governess or perhaps a teacher."

"I'm sure there's more than one man who would marry you."

Fine lines appeared at the corners of Isabelle's mouth as it turned up in amusement. "I haven't considered all my options."

Preach bit back a reply, He couldn't make an offer.

Her gaze dropped to the floor. "I just know I won't marry Daniel."

The dejection in her voice tore at his gut. She shouldn't have to stay in Stony Creek because she didn't have the money. He cleared his throat. "Does that mean you're going back to the camp? I could give you the funds to travel if you have somewhere else to go." Ever since he was saved, Preach had sent his pay to his ma for safekeeping, but Perley was always good for a loan, although his interest was steep. Some of the men owed him their whole paycheck by the time Joe Pollitt delivered the crisp bills of their wages to the bunkhouse.

"I'll go back to the camp." Plucking at the material of her skirt, she continued, "It's as good a place as any to figure out what I want to do next."

Knowing she chose to return to the camp stirred up lightness in his heart—a joy not burdened by guilt or shame. Isabelle may not be the woman for Preach, but it had been so long since he had felt anything other than temptation with the fairer sex, he'd given up hope that he could simply be happy just knowing them. His prayers must be having some effect.

Preach surrounded her gloved hands with one of his own and pressed. "I'll collect the horse and meet you at Miss Sophie's."

An hour later, Preach reined Rosie to a point half way up Cougar Ridge Mountain, where he and Isabelle dismounted. Preach never tired of the view. The sun reflected off the soft grays and browns of the surrounding shale faces as they gathered to magnificent peaks topped with white hats of snow. The valley spread in the dark greens of a forest thick with coniferous trees. Bright golds and oranges from the poplars' fall leaves blazed like a fire along the wide river, as blue as the sky, which flowed through Stony Creek and continued east across the broad valley.

The same river that took the camp's winter's worth of logs out to the sawmill. Several of the men would join the river drive in the spring. Preach had never felt the hankering to go along. He liked his summers back home on the small farm in Alberta his ma and pa had worked their whole lives.

"It's beautiful." Isabelle stared across the valley. "It almost makes you think…"

When she didn't finish, he turned to her. "Think what?" Standing here with Isabelle, watching her take in the view, he could almost believe in a future for the two of them—a cozy log cabin, several children playing by the hearth.

"I don't know, it's just beautiful."

He turned back to the vista. "This is my favorite spot and the best view along this road. Sometimes, when it gets to be too much, I ride out here and spend a couple of hours reading my Bible under a tree." It was true these days. Not always, though. There was a hollow, warmed by the sun and sheltered from the wind, which lay just below the edge of the point. Preach used to buy a bottle in town and drink it down in the hideaway so he wouldn't have to share it with the others.

Isabelle tipped her head back. Her gaze held a question. "When what gets to be too much?"

As she studied his face, his resolve melted. He drank in the delicate rise of her cheek bones, the soft curve of her lips, and leaned toward her.

"Preach?"

His head snapped back. What had he been thinking?

How much should he tell her? How long would it be before she figured it out on her own? He wasn't all that he made himself out to be, regardless of what the people of Stony Creek thought.

He struggled. He struggled hard against the temptations of his old life—the drink, the gambling, the women. Since he had come to know the Lord, there wasn't a day that went by Preach wasn't defending himself against the onslaught of the devil and his schemes. It wore on a man, and sometimes he needed time out of the fray, away from the men's rough talk and banter, so he wouldn't be drawn back in—another reason to find a suitable wife.

She didn't need to know all that. "The close quarters at the camp can get to you after a while."

Isabelle stared across the valley. "Things can get to you, all right."

"We should probably keep going. Your Aunt Lou won't rest until you turn up." Preach slung Isabelle up behind him on the saddle and tugged on the reins to back Rosie up before guiding her toward the rough road leading to the camp.

Fifteen minutes later, Rosie faltered on a steep incline along a game trail linking two broad curves in the road. Isabelle gasped before slinging her arms around Preach's waist.

"I think we're too much for the horse," she said.

Preach couldn't keep the corners of his mouth from turning up in a smile. A good thing Isabelle couldn't see it. She might not be the woman for him, but he'd been waiting for her to clamp on since they'd left town.

He reached out and smoothed the horse's mane. "You'll be fine won't you, girl?"

"Please let me off. The horse shouldn't have to suffer because I was impetuous."

Rosie turned her ears back and twitched them at the rise in Isabelle's pitch.

"Settle down. You're spooking her. This horse is use to hauling big loads, the two of us are no problem for her."

"Please. Let me get off and walk."

"It'll be another two hours if you get off now. We're just past half way."

"I don't care how far it is. I want to get off!" Isabelle pushed back from the saddle and motioned to sling her leg over.

What had gotten into her? Preach wrenched the reins, and the horse stopped. "Give me a minute, would you? You're going to hurt yourself." He dismounted from the horse and locked his fingers together. Isabelle slipped a boot into the support and descended. The girl weighed nothing at all.

After smoothing her skirt, she tossed her carpet bag over one shoulder and turned to walk up the snaked trail.

"I wish you'd get back on the horse. The going's a lot harder up hill."

"I'm sure I'll be fine."

Isabelle took two steps up the trail, her boot caught on a root, and she staggered sideways before landing in the underbrush and letting out a soft "ouch."

Preach lifted her to an upright position. "You hurt yourself?"

She huffed and yanked her arm out of his grip.

"Just let me be." Isabelle straightened her narrow shoulders and continued up the trail.

After wrapping Rosie's reins around a fist, he followed, but before rounding the next bend, her skirt caught up in a wild rose bush encroaching on the path. She tugged it away, snapping several branches, and almost lost her footing once more.

How could he let her be? The woman *was* going to hurt herself, it was obvious she had no experience walking bush trails. She'd most likely twist her ankle, if not worse. "Look, let's get back up on the horse. Rosie can walk these trails better than you can."

Isabelle shook her head and picked up her pace.

What was her problem? Rosie had simply stumbled earlier. It happened all the time on the rough terrain. "It'll save a lot of wear and tear on your dress." And keep Preach from feeling guilty about letting her walk.

Isabelle didn't look back as she responded. "I'll worry about my dress, thank you."

"Look, trust me, the horse will be fine. We'll be fine."

Isabelle stopped abruptly and made a slow arc to face him. She glared up at him, her lips flattened into a line as if she were angry. "I will forever regret the last time I trusted a man."

~

*I*sabelle's heart thumped a wild beat in her chest as she challenged Preach on the pathetic trail in the middle of nowhere. Anger coursed through every vein. She wanted to scream, to kick a nearby tree, or to throw something like the thick chunk of broken branch not two feet from the trail.

It wouldn't do any good. At least it never had. Since the night Daniel had taken advantage of her, she never knew when the anger would strike, and its vehemence always caught her off guard. She hadn't meant to say what she felt out loud, though, and Preach looked confused. No one had heard her speak—not her parents, not even Kittie—about what bothered Isabelle most concerning the night of the May Ball.

She had trusted Daniel, and he had betrayed that trust.

Preach stared back at her as if she'd lost her mind, and maybe she had. It wasn't his fault—being a man.

Even if he was a pastor, Isabelle didn't know him overly well.

A man could say anything in a bunch of letters. By leaving town with him—alone—she'd made herself vulnerable again. She should have stayed in town with Miss Sophie for a couple of days until Aunt Lou had come to get the mail. When would she learn?

Preach tugged the reins, urging the horse to follow him up the path.

"Go on ahead," she said. The idea of walking back alone wasn't appealing, particularly the nearer it came to sunset, but at least Isabelle wouldn't have to explain why she had gotten angry.

He froze, turned to her. "There's no way I'm leaving you to walk back to the camp alone. It wasn't safe when you left this morning, either."

Isabelle planted her feet on the trail as Preach and the horse sauntered toward her. "I made it didn't I? And I will again."

"If you're so sure of everything, then maybe you can tell me what your aunt is going to do to me when I show up at the camp and tell her I left you in the woods to make your way back."

He had a point. There were bound to be repercussions already for taking off the way she had. And, considering the telegram, the repercussions wouldn't involve Aunt Lou sending Isabelle home. "Fine. I don't feel comfortable on the horse, I'm walking. You do as you please." Her foot faltered on a root as she turned and started up the trail.

Preach and the horse fell in behind her.

Five minutes later, they arrived at the road and continued walking for over an hour without speaking. Preach's long legs kept pace with Isabelle's, and the horse followed a few lengths behind.

"We should stop and have some water," he said. "We've got another hour to go."

Isabelle licked her lips. She *was* thirsty.

Preach fetched his canteen from the saddle bag, unscrewed the lid, and offered it to her. She took several long sips before handing it back.

Preach held her gaze as he tipped the canteen back and swallowed. After wiping his mouth, he replaced the lid. "Any chance you might explain what happened back there?"

It was none of his business. She could tell him that or she could tell him she didn't want to talk about it. Either response would probably shut the inquiry down. He hadn't pressed her until now, which said a lot about the man's patience and his character. Maybe it was time she finally told someone.

Preach had meant to kiss her when they'd stopped to take in the view back down the trail—before she'd interrupted him. Perhaps he did feel something for her. And for a brief moment, when his handsome face had bent toward hers, she'd welcomed it. Until his face had turned into Daniel's and Isabelle's breakfast had threatened to spill from her throat and onto the ground.

Preach already knew there was a reason Isabelle's father had sent her to the camp. Aunt Lou had made sure of that. And now that he had seen the telegram, he would be putting a story together in his head. Isabelle might as well give him the right one. Her tale would take care of any future thoughts Preach had about kissing her and protect his reputation from being sullied by the likes of her, too.

Isabelle gestured for Preach to pass the canteen over again. The cool water barely touched the burn building in her throat. She bent and coughed.

"You all right?"

Isabelle straightened and wiped her mouth on her sleeve. There was no way she was telling him the story face to face. "I'm fine." She rotated to continue walking up the road. "My father sent me here hoping I would recuperate and also hoping I would bend to his will."

"I figured it probably had something to do with Daniel and your not wanting to marry him."

"I supposed you might, from the telegram." Isabelle waited for Preach to make a further comment, anything that might ease her into what she was about to say. His steps continued to crunch on the mixed stone and clay of the road, but he didn't utter a word.

"I couldn't marry Daniel, not after he…" Her courage faltered. She took a deep breath, tried again. "I've been sick since the spring, barely able to leave my room." And even when Isabelle felt well enough to leave, she didn't want to. "My family tried various cures, but none of them worked." How could they work when her illness wasn't physical?

"Hmm."

The man wasn't making the telling easy. "My father was worried about how thin I'd grown and Aunt Lou was his last resort." Isabelle lifted her skirt and let it drop. "I used to actually fill out my clothes. I lost my appetite after…the incident." Incident—a tidy, sterile word for what Daniel had done. "Coming to the camp has helped, partly because she's worked me so hard and partly because her cooking is so delicious. For the first two days, I lay in bed, just like I had at home. And then Aunt Lou said there would be 'no more of that.' The next morning, she hauled me out to the kitchen counter to peel a bucket of potatoes. I didn't think I would ever get through them. It took me half the day." Two weeks later, Isabelle could peel the same amount in a quarter of the time.

Maybe Father *had* been correct in sending Isabelle to her aunt.

"Your aunt is a force to be reckoned with. And the incident?"

Isabelle tipped her head back and stared into the deep green of the forest lining the road. Her stomach rolled and pitched. "I-I made a grave mistake in judgment."

The horse's hooves clip clopped on the road behind her.

"I never should have gotten into the carriage."

A hawk screamed as it dipped and soared on an air current above their heads. She flinched at the sound.

"What happened?" Preach's voice was soft—understanding.

She couldn't look at him. "I was taken advantage of." Isabelle's voice dropped away as she spoke the words. They walked on for several paces. "I knew it was wrong to get in the carriage unescorted with Daniel, but I trusted him."

If Isabelle had done the right thing in the first place, Daniel's indiscretion never would have happened. The familiar shame tingled both her cheeks. "That wasn't the end of it either. One of the girls in my circle of friends discovered something had happened and took great delight in sharing her version of the event."

She closed her eyes to fight the memory away, but its clutches pulled her in.

Isabelle turned the tap and wrung her hands as the cold water poured over them for several minutes. She then splashed water over her face. Who cared about the skillfully applied face powder, lip stain, and light brown eyeshadow?

Her legs throbbed. She lifted her petticoat, crinoline, and tugged at her monogrammed drawers, which fell in a torn and bloodied heap to the floor. She kicked them into the corner before a sob escaped her lips. Using a cloth from the cabinet, Isabelle rubbed the inside of her thighs until angry welts appeared. Why had he done it? As far as both families were concerned, it was only a matter of time before Isabelle and Daniel would have been married.

Isabelle collapsed on the toilet and dropped her head. Her shoulders shook as she wept.

When a knock sounded, she jumped.

Please go away.

"Are you all right?"

Stella, the last girl Isabelle wanted to see. Isabelle pressed her eyes and steadied her voice. "If you could give me a few moments."

"Isabelle, is that you? I wish I could. I've been waiting out here for ten minutes and... Well, you know with our corsets extra tight."

Isabelle looped the rinsed cloth over the brass towel holder before opening the door.

CHAPTER 9

*T*he truth was just as Preach had feared. He dropped his head and scrubbed his fingers across his brows. Regret filled his chest. "Lord, she's no kind of wife for a pastor."

Isabelle gasped.

Oh, Lord. He'd not meant to speak those words aloud. The tears trailing down her cheeks jerked at his heart. If he could, he would grab the words he'd muttered and toss them under the horse's hooves.

No other words passed between them on the remaining journey to the camp. When they arrived, Isabelle veered toward the cook shack, shoulders slumped.

He'd added to her burden.

Preach led Rosie toward the corral. "You deserve some grain and a good brushing down don't you, girl." He pulled the saddle from the horse's back and slung it over one of the crude partitions separating the stalls. "Although, you're probably wondering why Isabelle and I walked half the way home. Isabelle was afraid, but it's not your fault." He pulled the blanket off and tossed it beside the saddle before reaching under Rosie's forelock and rubbing the white patch above her eyes. Rosie dropped her head and pressed her nose against Preach's chest.

"Whose fault is it?"

Preach whirled around. Snoop leaned against the door frame of the barn, arms crossed and a scowl pulling at the corners of his mouth.

"Whose fault is what?" As usual, the man's questions got under Preach's skin.

"That Isabelle was afraid."

Preach turned from Snoop to remove Rosie's bridle. Isabelle's story was none of Snoop's business. It wasn't Preach's business either, he'd already decided they couldn't marry before he knew the details.

It was the thing he liked least about being a pastor. It sure didn't feel like a privilege to carry around the sordid details of other people's lives. They laid heavy on his heart. *Lord, forgive me.* He had enough sordid details in his own life he wanted to forget.

"I suppose you'll have to ask Isabelle about that," Preach said, "if Lou will let you anywhere near her." Not likely, at least she shouldn't. Snoop had no respect for women, even if he could put on a good enough show to get what he desired. Preach's conscience took a jab at his thoughts. It hadn't been all that long since he'd behaved the same way. Preach hung the bridle on a nail by the others and picked up the curry comb.

"Did her being afraid have anything to do with you?"

Preach's hand stilled on the horse's withers. "What are you implying?"

"I ain't implying anything. I'm just asking. You're a pretty imposing figure."

Preach continued brushing the chestnut brown of the horse's coat. "Imposing, am I? I didn't know you felt that way, Snoop." The man had a hot temper. The words just might be enough to make him storm off and leave Preach alone.

Snoop guffawed.

Guess not.

"Your size don't mean anything to me, but it might to a woman."

Snoop's comments were no longer about Isabelle, and it was about time Snoop let it go. Preach hadn't gone sniffing around Lavinia *once* since he'd been saved—nor did he intend to in the future. He'd left that life behind, Lord willing. Snoop could have Lavinia all to himself. Preach turned to look Snoop straight on. "Is this about Isabelle or—?"

"What did you do, Preach?"

Preach's fist tightened around the handle of the comb. It wouldn't be the first time he and Snoop had gone at it. The man was meaner than a snake and just as wily. Snoop would get in some good licks, Preach didn't care if he did.

Lord, give me patience. It wouldn't help Isabelle's heartache any if Snoop and Preach roughed each other up.

"How long did it take you to find her?"

Preach laughed. "A whole lot less longer than it took you. I spotted her in town before noon."

"Noon. Why'd it take you so long to get back here?"

Air filled Preach's lungs as he pulled a slow breath between his teeth. "Don't you have somewhere to be? How are the men in the bunkhouse doing?"

"You weren't too worried about the men when you took your sweet time getting back."

The men had crossed his mind once or twice, but it wasn't as if much was going to change whether Preach had been here or not. Spending time with Isabelle had been a welcome shift from the bunch of whiners.

"You folks take a detour?"

Snoop had gone too far. Preach turned and took a step forward, raising his fist.

"Charles Thaddeus Bailey." Lou marched into the barn, her

arms jutting out from her hips. "You'll lower that fist right now, if you know what's good for you."

Apparently Alvin couldn't keep a secret. Preach had shared with him one night around the fire how Preach's mother insisted on naming her boys after the twelve apostles. There wasn't a ma in the whole country happier that one of her sons was preaching the gospel than his ma.

After catching the smirk that flashed across Snoop's face, Preach stepped back. Rosie whinnied and turned to nudge his shoulder.

"What's going on in here?" Lou asked.

"I've just been asking Preach where he and your niece were all afternoon," Snoop said. "I covered the country three times over in the time it took for them to get back to the camp. I was getting worried. I thought maybe something had happened to her."

Snoop was more likely to be worried about whether Isabelle would come back so he could collect his winnings.

Lou's dark eyes stared into Preach's. "Did he answer your question?"

Another smirk. "Nope, maybe you can get some answers. She's *your* niece."

"Well, Preach," Lou said, "why don't you tell us where you and my niece have been all day? And then you can tell us why she walked into the cook shack with tears running down her cheeks. The poor girl didn't speak a word before she locked herself away in her room."

Preach had disappointed Isabelle, but he wasn't the only one. "Why did she take off in the first place, Lou?"

Lou's nostrils flared.

She could be as tough as one of the men. Preach would be in trouble if Lou and Snoop decided to hang a lickin' on him.

"You can thank me for finding her and bringing her home when you get around to it," Preach added. "One of your mincemeat pies should take care of it." Preach turned back to the horse so he wouldn't see the expression on Lou's face, which was guaranteed to be loaded with guilt. There was no need for her to see the same look on his face. She could stew for a while and believe Isabelle's sorrow was all her own doing.

A minute later, Lou still hadn't come up with a retort. Preach continued to brush the horse.

"Lou, are you going to let Preach get away with this?" Snoop demanded. "Maybe we should bring Isabelle over and find out why she's so upset."

"Let the girl be, Snoop," Preach's words held as much warning as he could give them.

"Why should I?"

"She's feeling poorly enough without us asking her all kinds of questions."

Lou sighed. "Why did she come back, Preach?" she asked, her voice heavy. "I'm assuming she made it to town, and once she got that far..."

"She sent a telegram, and her pa said she couldn't come home." It was up to Isabelle to tell her aunt the condition of being allowed to rejoin the family. Not that it mattered. According to Isabelle, she wasn't going to marry Daniel. A fact that relieved him more than it should.

"I thought as much. Look, most of the men are feeling a lot better. I imagine their appetites will be returning, and they'll be clamoring for food by morning. I'm going back to the cook shack. I'll leave the two of you to take care of them. There's a cold plate for you in the dining room, Preach. "

"That's it? You're not going to get to the bottom of why Preach and Isabelle have been gone so long, Lou?"

"You heard me," Lou said. "The men need taking care of."

"But—"

"You're needed in the bunkhouse." The sounds of Lou's footsteps faded away after she left the barn.

Preach smiled as he patted Rosie's side. It was about time Snoop didn't get his way. Lou seemed to have a soft spot for the man—annoying as he was.

Preach would give the horse some grain before he went to the dining room. The bunkhouse could wait. "Don't let me hold you up," he said to Snoop as he slid a halter over Rosie's nose.

Snoop mumbled something Preach didn't catch and stomped out of the barn.

Fifteen minutes later, Preach stepped over the threshold into the bunkhouse. It was a whole different scene from what it had been over the last week. All but Mack were dressed and either reclining on their bunks or talking with the others. If you looked past all the faded spots and crusted blisters around their mouths and on their hands, it looked like business as usual. A good thing, Preach was tired of being their nursemaid.

"Here he is, boys, the other hero," Will called out from his bunk.

The men cheered and clapped, yelling out Preach's name as he tugged the door closed. Preach extended his arm toward the men. "I don't think I did any more than what the rest of you would have done." Dropping his arm to his side, he continued. "I'm glad to see most of you are feeling better." He glanced at Mack, lying still, eyes closed, and blanket pulled up to his chin. "It's been a long week."

"A week!" Horace's thick eyebrows shot up his forehead. "We've been down for a week?"

Snoop strutted to the center of the bunkhouse. "Six days, and me and Preach have been here taking care of you for every one of them. Except today." Snoop glared at Preach. "Why don't you tell the men where you were this afternoon? I'd be interested in knowing myself."

The men's gazes swung to Preach as if they were watching a trapeze artist.

"I went to town. Snoop's sore because he went the wrong way and wandered around in the woods."

"Went the wrong way for what?" Snoop asked.

He had him there. Preach cleared his throat and sat on his bunk. "I'm tired." He stretched, grazing the ceiling, and followed the stretch with an exaggerated yawn. Maybe the men would grant him mercy and let the telling go.

"I guess he's not going to tell you, Preach was chasing the wood nymph."

The room gave a collective gasp, and the men's necks twisted as they looked from one to another, some shrugging.

"You mean she's real?" Perley asked. "Is that true?"

He had the most to lose, his odds were four to one she didn't exist. "Maybe." Preach slipped his boots off while the room filled with *I knew its* and *It's not possibles*.

"Lou's been hiding her niece in the cook shack," Snoop said. "The girl took off this morning, and Lou asked us to go find her. That's who I saw the other night." He held his palm out toward Perley. "Time to pay up."

You gotta be joshing." Unbelief raising the pitch in Will's voice.

It *was* hard to wrap one's mind around the thought. From what Preach could tell, there was no family resemblance between Lou and Isabelle. For that matter, it was hard to imagine Lou had ever been young, let alone pretty. How could he tell the men about Isabelle without getting them all worked up? If he mentioned the intelligent brown eyes above a narrow nose and plump lips, they were likely to form a line at Lou's back door, hoping for a glimpse. Isabelle didn't need that kind of attention.

"Let's talk about it in the morning," Preach said.

"I don't think so." The corner of Snoop's lip curled up in a sneer as he shook his head. "You've been calling me a liar for two weeks."

Preach hadn't called Snoop a liar once. It was hardly Preach's fault if the men had let their imaginations get the better of them. With months on end at the camp and only each other as companions, the men were easily given over to suggestion just to keep from going stir crazy.

All eyes were on Preach—some hopeful, some worried. More than likely, the worried ones were those who had bet more than they should have on what they thought was a sure thing. Why hadn't they learned by now? Preach should plan a sermon on the fruit of self-control and drag some of these sorry creatures to one of the church benches to listen with the rest of the congregation.

"Lou's niece has been helping her in the cook shack," Preach said.

"What did I tell ya?" Snoop whooped, and the bunkhouse filled with the jabber of the men.

Preach lay back on his bed during the ruckus and laced his fingers behind his head. What he wouldn't give to shut his eyes and sleep the night through. His eyes fluttered closed.

Before sleep could overtake him, something thumped on Preach's forehead. His eyes blinked open to see a rolled ball of wool socks beside him on the bunk. He picked it up and turned it. The neat stitches along the curve of the big toe meant they could only be Ernie's. He'd escaped the confines of his father's tailor shop four years ago to make it big in the lumber industry. The fact that Ernie was still rooming with nineteen other men in a shack that stunk like his socks was a testament to how the decision had worked out for him.

Ernie eyed him from his bunk across the room. "What does she look like? Is she tall and beautiful with hair down to her knees like Snoop said?"

Preach chucked the ball back at Ernie. He ducked, and it bounced on the wall knocking off a piece of bark before landing behind him.

What could Preach say? That she was the most beautiful woman he'd ever had the privilege of meeting? That looking in her sorrow-filled eyes sucked the oxygen out of his chest and made him want to beat the face of a man named Daniel to a pulp?

What he thought of Isabelle didn't matter anymore. She wasn't the kind of woman a pastor could marry. She was soiled.

For some reason, the thought of letting this gang of riffraff at Isabelle still irked. "The girl's sick."

Snoop's gaze snapped in Preach's direction.

"Is that true, Snoop, or is he just trying to put us off?" Will asked.

"I don't know. I've never met her. I just know what I saw in the moonlight. She looked pretty good to me." He raised an eyebrow, challenging Preach.

It wouldn't hurt to give the men some of the facts. It might help cool their ardor. "Her father, Lou's brother, sent her to the camp to convalesce."

"Why in tarnation would he send her here? This is no place to recuperate," Horace said. "The way Lou works in the kitchen, she'll be lucky to survive, let alone restore her health."

Several of the men laughed.

The fact that Isabelle had been sent to the camp showed how desperate her father had been to secure her marriage to Daniel.

"She single?" Will asked. "Is that why Lou's keeping her a secret?"

If the men discovered Isabelle was even a possibility for a romantic entanglement, there would be no end of trouble. Isabelle wouldn't have a moment's peace, and Joe would be obliged to send her from the camp. Preach wasn't ready to see Isabelle leave even knowing there could no longer be a relationship between the two of them. He fixed his features into a mask before responding. "I already told you, she's sick."

"Sick with what?" Snoop asked.

Over Preach's dead body would Snoop be attempting to woo the girl. The rivalry over Lavinia had nothing to do with Isabelle, and Preach would make sure Snoop knew that. Besides, Preach's interest in Lavinia was over—she was Snoop's now. "It's Isabelle's business what she's sick with."

"Isabelle? Now that's a pretty name," Alvin said, his lips turning up into a lewd grin.

Drat. He shouldn't have said that. Now the men would have a name to attach their imaginings to. "Look, all I know is that Lou thought the fresh air and water up here would do her some good. The last thing she needs is for a bunch of lonely men to bother her, so forget she's here. It's nine o'clock, lights out." Preach rolled over on to his side, indicating the conversation's end.

The men retired to their beds, and the lanterns were snuffed. Preach plumped his pillow to the murmured conversations going on between the bunks.

"Preach," Snoop said as Preach's eyes were closing.

"What?"

"I'm just wondering something."

Of course Snoop was wondering something, he never stopped wondering. "What's that?"

"Does not bothering Isabelle include you?"

The answer to that question was none of Snoop's business, either. "Get some sleep."

CHAPTER 10

*R*olling over, Isabelle groaned and tightened the warm quilt around her shoulders. Aunt Lou's knock on the bedroom door had come much too early for the number of hours Isabelle could count as last night's sleep. And if the ropes tightening around her calves were an indicator, stepping to the cold floor would be painful.

Why had she insisted on walking halfway up the mountain the day before? The horse's stumbling had made Isabelle anxious, but it was more than that. Spending time with Preach, she had almost felt safe—until he'd said "trust me."

At Preach's words, a memory had swooped in. Daniel's eyes —cold, emotionless—boring into hers before he'd leaned in and trailed kisses across one collarbone. Kisses she'd resisted. Isabelle had shoved against Daniel's chest, but he'd been more solid than she expected. He merely laughed at her attempt to push him away before pinning her arms against the carriage bench and bending toward her once more. "Trust me," he'd murmured against her skin as the buttons from the tufted cushion dug into her spine. "You'll be fine."

Isabelle had not been fine. Would she ever be fine again?

Thanks to her decision to share Daniel's behavior with Preach, Isabelle had witnessed the demise of her reputation in another person's eyes. It hadn't been Preach's fault he looked at her the way he did. Isabelle couldn't fault a pastor for his judgment.

Although Isabelle didn't fault him, Preach's comment about "her being no kind of a wife for a pastor" had stung her heart like a hot iron. The tears she'd shed walking to the cook shack hadn't soothed the burn either.

When Isabelle had stepped inside the back door, mercifully, Aunt Lou's open mouth had closed without scolding. Nor had she protested when Isabelle escaped to her room without a word.

Aunt Lou wasn't likely to let Isabelle get away completely without punishment for running off. The dressing down would come today.

She sat up, slung her legs over the edge of the bed, and stepped to the floor. It was cold as ice, and she scurried to the desk to retrieve her thick wool stockings.

A persistent knock thudded on the back door. Aunt Lou whispered something in response to the inaudible inquiry. It wasn't likely to be Preach asking after Isabelle. His parting words had left no room for the possibility he would change his mind about her.

It hadn't come as a surprise that a pastor wasn't interested in marrying someone who'd been sullied by another, but the fact still stung. The letters they'd shared, the relief in his eyes when he'd found her, if only it had been enough to overcome what had happened to her.

Isabelle laced her boots and threw on the day's clothes before washing her face in the cold water of the basin and braiding her hair.

Another knock came to the back door, and another hushed conversation followed.

It was unusual for the men to bother Lou before breakfast. Joe had informed Aunt Lou last night that the loggers would be eating on schedule today, and with mountains of eggs, flapjacks, and bacon to prepare, she was unlikely to bide any interruptions.

Isabelle tied a brown ribbon around the base of her second braid before leaving her room. She lifted the latch of the back door in response to another insistent knock.

"Don't open that." Aunt Lou snatched the broom leaning against the wall beside the cook stove.

Isabelle removed her hand from the latch as Aunt Lou stomped down the hall.

"There are apples to be peeled for pies." She pointed over her shoulder toward the large metal bowl, apples heaped over its rim, which sat on the table next to sixteen lumps of pie dough.

"Why all the knocking?"

"The men are feeling their oats, I guess, all but Mack, who's still suffering, the poor boy. The others will be back chopping tomorrow. It couldn't come soon enough." Aunt Lou waited until Isabelle picked up a paring knife and had begun peeling before cracking the door and slipping through the opening with the broom.

Seven peeled apples later, Aunt Lou returned, her cheeks flushed, wisps of gray hair loose about her ears. She tucked the broom back into place and crossed the floor to the pantry before pulling the baking soda tin from the shelf to mix the mornings flapjacks. "It's a wonder someone so small could cause such a heap of trouble," she said without turning from the shelf, her fingers lingering on the salt box.

Who was Aunt Lou referring to, Isabelle? Was this the scolding she was bound to receive? The blade of Isabelle's knife slipped from the apple and sliced into her thumb. "Ouch." She closed her eyes and pressed the tip of her thumb behind her front teeth. The sting of the cut pulsed across her palm.

Yes, Isabelle had caused Aunt Lou considerable worry by taking off from the camp the day before, but what did that have to do with Isabelle's size? She hadn't always been so narrow, flat. In fact, her curvaceous figure had drawn the attention of men since she was fifteen—not that it had done her any good.

"Let me see." Aunt Lou tugged at Isabelle's sleeve.

Isabelle removed her thumb from her mouth, and blood seeped from the half-inch cut.

As Aunt Lou pulled at the edges of the cut a drop of blood landed on the white of a curled apple peel and spread like a crimson blush.

Isabelle's stomach tilted.

"It's not deep," Lou said. "Squeeze your thumb, and I'll fetch some ointment and a bandage. We've a lot to accomplish today. The men will be more than hungry now that they feel better." Aunt Lou plodded to her room.

Isabelle stared at the swinging door separating the kitchen from the dining room. She was just as useless in the kitchen as she was everywhere else. When Isabelle had been a young teen, guests had been known to sneak from the parlor when Father requested she play the piano forte after a dinner party, and Mother had yet to hang one of Isabelle's misshapen embroidery projects in their home. It was a kindness of Aunt Lou to take Isabelle on at the camp. She was more of a burden than a help.

Aunt Lou returned with a tin of carbolic ointment and a narrow strip of white cotton. After wiping the blood from Isabelle's fingers, she smeared a generous glob of the ointment on the cut and wrapped Isabelle's thumb with the bandage. The scent of the cloves Aunt Lou chewed to cover the scent of her furtive cigar smoking stung Isabelle's nostrils.

"The men know you're here now, and the boss will be fuming."

"You can tell him you didn't hire me, since you're not paying me. Perhaps that will help."

"I'll be keeping the details of our arrangement to myself. But it won't matter now. Joe won't let you stay." Aunt Lou turned Isabelle's thumb to inspect her work. "He'll probably ship you out before nightfall. I guess you'll be getting your wish and leaving the camp. Your father will have to find somewhere else to send you."

She was no help to Lou, and the only person Isabelle would consider staying at the camp for no longer thought her worthy of his company, so why did the words pull the air from her chest?

Aunt Lou took a knife from the block and trimmed the tails of the bandage to stubs. "I'll roll the pastry. You keep peeling." She dusted a large circle of flour on the table. After pulling the rolling pin from two hooks on the wall, she rubbed it with flour and slapped one of the lumps of pie dough on top. She rolled the dough with brisk, expert strokes as Isabelle peeled several more apples.

Within minutes, Aunt Lou had rolled and pressed four pie crusts into pans. "The boys won't bother you before you leave if they know what's good for them."

"Who came to the door this morning?"

"You'd do better to ask who *didn't*. I don't know how you slept through the parade of knocks. It started up at seven. Every single one of them was asking about the girl working in the kitchen. What color's her hair? How long is it? Does she sing? A couple of them asked something about a wood nymph. Is there something about you I don't know?"

"I'm not a wood nymph."

The rolling pin clattered to the table as Aunt Lou faced her, her floured hands gripped each side of her waist. Her dark eyes held something Isabelle couldn't read. "Young lady, I don't need you getting cocky with me. I've risked my livelihood by taking in a—" Her lips worked against each other as though deciding what definition would best suit Isabelle.

Isabelle hung her head and pushed down on the tears pressing at the base of her throat. "A what, Aunt Lou?" she whispered. "Go ahead and say it. What did Father say I was?"

"Self-pity won't get you anywhere with me. You've been moping for six months. Look at you. Has it done any good?"

Aunt Lou was known for her bluntness, but until this moment she'd never been outright mean. Isabelle lifted her chin to reply. "What are you hoping I'll say?"

"That you're sorry for causing your mother and father so much worry by almost starving yourself to death over a man."

The accusation brought a vise grip to Isabelle's chest. She had lost her appetite after Daniel's attack, but surely her family didn't believe Isabelle was *purposely* starving herself to death because of him. "You have no cause to say that."

"Don't I? It's about time someone voiced what everyone else is thinking."

How dare Aunt Lou speak for everyone? Scooping a handful of apple slices from the table Isabelle plopped them into one of the bottom pie crusts. "How would you know what they're all thinking, tucked up here, hidden away from the world like a recluse."

Aunt Lou crossed her arms, and the flour stamped the navy blue of her wool sleeves with prints. "I'll tell you how I know. Your mother has been writing to me for months. 'Please take in my wayward daughter.'" Aunt Lou's voice mimicked Isabelle's mother's genteel accent. "'We've tried everything. We don't know how to help her.'"

Although Isabelle had retreated to the confines of her room in the days following the May ball, Mother had appeared satisfied with the explanation Isabelle was upset at the demise of her relationship with Daniel. Mother hadn't pressed her for particulars, and Isabelle had been relieved to not have to share what Daniel had done. She'd never alluded to Isabelle being wayward or fearing for her life.

And when Daniel had been bold enough to come to their home two days after the May ball, Isabelle's mother had sent him away. Mother wouldn't have called her *wayward*. Mother wouldn't have begged Aunt Lou to take her. "I don't believe you."

Aunt Lou shrugged. "It doesn't matter if you believe me. After today, I won't have to worry about minding you anymore."

They finished the eight pies without another word. Aunt Lou slid them into the oven before ordering Isabelle to mix up the batter for the morning's flapjacks. For the next half hour, Isabelle slid one fluffy round circle after another from the grill and then onto platters resting under upturned bowls on the counter.

Aunt Lou finished the other food preparations and served the men when the tread of twenty pairs of boots echoed on the dining room floor. After refusing Isabelle's offer to help carry in the heaping platters, she slammed a serving fork down on the table and muttered something about the fact that Isabelle had caused enough trouble already.

The boss must have decided to let the men talk over today's breakfast. The jabber coming through the door was lively and interspersed with raucous laughter. Isabelle's name peppered several of the stories, the details of which were inaudible as she scrubbed and rinsed the morning's pots in the dishpans.

Aunt Lou shouldered through the dining room door carrying a bucket overflowing with the last of the dirty dishes. As she plunked it on the counter, a tin plate clattered to the floor. Isabelle's hands stilled in the steaming water.

"The boss wants to talk to me in his office. He's heard the story of the beautiful woman I've kept captive in the kitchen." Aunt Lou's laughter was not in amusement. "My very own Cinderella."

Isabelle bit her tongue. Aunt Lou's jutting chin and glaring eyes were not inviting a challenge.

Her aunt untied her apron from her waist and hung it on the hook by the back door. "I'm going over to the office. I can't do anything about you staying here at the camp any longer, but you and your father better hope I still have a job when I return."

Isabelle let the latch snick before drying her hands and stepping to the pantry shelves. On her tiptoes, she removed the cracker tin from the top shelf. Inside the tin lay a stack of letters, many of their edges worn and browned. Isabelle flipped through the stack looking for Mother's fanciful handwriting.

Four letters deep, she pulled the familiar ivory letterhead with delicate daisies trailing across the top from the tin. July fifteenth stared back at Isabelle from the top of the page. Over three months ago, Aunt Lou hadn't been lying.

July 15, 1898

Dearest Lou,

I trust my letter finds you in good health. Should you decide to take a break and much deserved rest from your labors at the logging camp, please know the door to our home is always open.

I'm taking the initiative to write to you in hopes you will be able to help us. My Dear Alexander has allowed my correspondence to you; however, I fear he has given up on Isabelle and believes neither you nor anyone else can help her.

Our precious daughter languishes day after day in her room. She will take only the barest of sustenance and has grown impossibly thin. We all fear for her life.

For months Isabelle had preferred the solitude of her room. Hiding away seemed like a better option than rousing her energy to walk out the door and perhaps see Daniel. Isabelle never wanted to face him again.

But even in the darkest days, her own death had never felt like a solution to her pain, and she'd never wished to slip its black cloak around her shoulders. How Mother must have suffered with her worry.

The cause is not an uncommon one...

Isabelle's brow wrinkled at the words. Not an uncommon cause? Were young women regularly accosted by the men they trusted?

...under the pressure of a young man, a young man we wholly approved of, our daughter put herself in a compromising situation, and unfortunately one of our deepest fears was realized.

Even more appalling, one of the local girls discovered the couple's indiscretion and has taken great joy to ensure Isabelle's reputation was completely sullied.

Stella had indeed taken great joy in spreading the story of the evidence she'd found to prove her belief Daniel and Isabelle had engaged in a romantic tryst.

The young man in question has returned to our home several times to express his sorrow over the occurrence and request our forgiveness. We had hoped that, given time, Isabelle would overcome her shame and sorrow to resume her relationship with the young man, who intends to marry her. Alexander feels it would make the best of a difficult situation.

However, Isabelle will not listen to reason and refuses to see him.

Of course Isabelle refused to see Daniel. What a scoundrel. He hadn't admitted to her parents he forced himself on her, or they would have thrown him out. But Mother was right about one thing—the incident had indeed been Isabelle's fault. She was the one who climbed into the carriage without a chaperone.

If you would be kind enough to allow our wayward daughter to come and work with you. I hope the change of scenery will restore her health and spirits and also encourage her to comply with her father's wishes.

My sincerest regards,

Emily Franklin

Daniel had misrepresented what he'd done. It was no marvel Isabelle's parents expected her to marry him. If she had known how they were being manipulated, Isabelle would have overcome her reluctance and told them the whole story.

Daniel, Father, Preach—even Joe. Why should they decide what Isabelle did and didn't do? By her own choice, she would stay at the camp and help Aunt Lou until she fully recuperated, and then *Isabelle* would decide where she went next.

Pulling the collar of her coat up around her cheeks, she marched from the cook shack to the camp office, ignoring the comments and catcalls from the men loitering around the bunkhouse. They, too, would have to get used to her presence at the camp—single woman or not.

At Isabelle's knock on the rough door, a gruff voice bid her enter.

A broad-shouldered burly man with a mop of black locks and a broad nose sat at a narrow desk. Tidy stacks of paper lay on its surface below a calendar tacked to the wall where a scantily clad woman looked back over her shoulder as she walked a tightrope carrying a frilled parasol. Isabelle averted her eyes.

"You must be the woman Lou's been hiding away from us. Isabelle is it?" He crossed his arms and leaned back to tip the front legs of his chair back before taking Isabelle in from head to toe.

"Isabelle, leave." Aunt Lou sat across from the man, head down, picking at a spot of sap on the lap of her dress.

"You said she was your niece." A slow smile spread across the man's face. "I can't say as I see much resemblance."

"She'll be gone shortly. She can walk down the mountain and catch the train today." Aunt Lou glanced at Isabelle from the corner of her eye. "She's done it before. I'm sorry for all the trouble she's caused, Joe."

The train would run through Stony Creek today, but it wouldn't be taking Isabelle with it.

Joe sniggered. "I'm surprised you could keep her hidden this long. But I agree, she'll have to leave." He dropped the chair legs to the floor, picked up a fountain pen, and commenced entering a number in a column book.

"I would like to stay," Isabelle said.

"You're not staying," Aunt Lou snapped before dropping her gaze to her lap again.

Isabelle squared her shoulders. "I would like to stay, sir."

The man's pen paused, and a drop of ink dripped from the tip obscuring the last number he'd written in the column. "Blast." He dabbed the spot with a blotter before turning toward Isabelle, his scraggly eyebrows pulled into a deep furrow. "Perhaps I'm mistaken. The girl appears to be more like you than I thought, Lou. She's got the same spunk you had that first summer. How old are you, miss?"

"Seven—"

"She's not staying." Aunt Lou had twisted the lap of her dress into both fists and was squeezing it with whitened knuckles.

"She's older than you were at Bear's Paw."

He swung an arm out to take in the shack. Along the back wall a small fire blazed in a stone fireplace. Several feet away, a narrow bed with a smooth red wool blanket stretched under a small window. At the head of the bed, a wooden stump served as a bedside table, where a copy of Walden rested next to a lamp. "You appear to be a woman used to finer surroundings." With two fingers he supported his chin as though working something out in his mind before continuing. "The work days are long. Although, I've been informed you've been here for two weeks"—he glanced at her aunt—"so you must know that by now. I'm not sure *why* you would want to stay."

"I've nowhere else to go."

He laughed. "You could have said you loved the work."

"She can go home," Aunt Lou said.

Isabelle took a step toward Joe. If she went, wherever it was, it would be Isabelle's decision. "Please believe me when I say, sir, I have nowhere else to go. Yes, the work is hard, but it's done me a lot of good. Ask Aunt Lou."

"Send her home," Lou said. "She's already caused enough trouble with the men."

"I promise, you won't regret letting me stay. I will not encourage any attention from the men."

He rested his forearms on the desk. "The girl says she's got nowhere to go, Lou. I'll speak to the men, and I'll threaten them with firing if they bother you, but like you said, it will be up to you not to encourage their attention. I won't tolerate bedlam at this camp."

"But—"

"Lou, give the girl a chance. I never regretted giving you one."

CHAPTER 11

*P*reach slapped the reins against the horse's backs to speed their pace down the rutted road toward Stony Creek, even though the narrow wheel base of Joe's buggy caused Isabelle to knock against his shoulder constantly. The experience wasn't an unpleasant one.

He'd been taken aback when Isabelle had agreed to attend church with him. Since their conversation on the trip home from town three days before, he'd taken her aside and apologized for speaking so bluntly. She'd said she understood his convictions about the kind of girl he should marry, and they had agreed to remain friends.

Only friends. As much as his head told him that was best, he couldn't seem to convince his heart. But at least she hadn't left the camp.

How Isabelle had convinced Joe to let her stay on as assistant cook was a complete mystery. Lou had been muttering under her breath about it ever since.

"I'll admit, you're good for business." Preach looked out the back window to eye the wagon of men following them down Cougar Ridge Mountain.

Isabelle coughed politely and rearranged her skirt to cover the toes of her boots, a fruitless gesture as, once again, a deep rut threatened to bounce her out the side of the buggy. She clutched his sleeve for an instant.

"It's a wonder Joe let you stay on after he found out Lou was hiding you away in the kitchen. What did you promise him?"

A gasp could be heard over the rumble of the wheels.

Preach could slap himself. Everything he said to the woman this morning was the wrong thing. "That didn't sound like I meant it to." His gaze darted to Isabelle. "I was just wondering..."

"What, Preach? What were you wondering?" Isabelle's brown eyes searched his.

What were they looking for, encouragement? He couldn't give it. Preach turned back to the road before clearing his throat. "It's just that Joe likes to follow the rule of no marriageable women working at the camp."

Isabelle turned to stare down the road, and her voice slipped to a whisper. "Like you said the other day, I pretty much fit the description of that kind of woman."

"You know that's not what I was saying. Any one of the buffoons behind us would be happy to marry—"

Isabelle pressed her mouth into a tight line.

Drat, he'd done it again.

"Any chance I can join you two up there?" Will called out from the wagon. "It'll be a bit tight, but it might keep the pretty lady from bouncing over the side. Your driving could use some refining, Preach." Will's high pitched laughter reverberated off the thick bank of pines lining the road and began a rash of opinions on Preach's driving from the other men in the wagon.

As they died down, Alvin called out, "I could drive you, Miss Isabelle. It wouldn't be no problem for me."

"Until you take a bath, Alvin, no woman wants to come within six feet of you," Perley said, and the others agreed.

"Preach isn't looking for our help, boys," Snoop said. "He's happy enough to have the lady to himself."

"It's a fair enough exchange, you warrant?" Preach called over his shoulder.

Snoop could be heard growling his displeasure to the other men.

"Exchange for what?" Isabelle asked.

It wasn't an exchange, nor was it a comparison. As Preach had tactlessly mentioned the other day, Isabelle wasn't marrying material for him, but he couldn't resist having one up on Snoop. The man always thought he had everything figured out. "It's just a little friendly banter between me and Snoop."

"I would never have taken you two for friends."

Isabelle had only observed Snoop and Preach during a couple of meals, but anybody who spent more time with them would know how deep the animosity ran.

"Hang on," Preach said. "We're going to put a little distance between ourselves and the wagon. I need to be at the church a few minutes early, prepare some people for the rowdies behind us."

Isabelle gripped the side of the buggy as Preach slapped the reigns, and they bounced and jostled down the rough clay and rocks.

Ten minutes later, Preach pulled the buggy to a stop in front of a low hedge of caragana bushes running parallel to Stony Creek Chapel. Situated just outside of town, the church had been built five years ago, the white clapboard siding on the rectangular building looked bright and fresh. The bell tower above the front door boasted cedar shingles, and a tall cross rose from its roof point. The cross doubled as a lightning rod owing to the fact that the last church building had burned down during a violent spring storm.

"What a pretty little church," she said. "It's absolutely stunning tucked into the evergreens like it is."

Preach rounded the buggy to assist her descent. "It's tiny, all right, and a small congregation, too, normally no more than thirty or so of us. I'm not sure where we'll put the extra men. I'll have to let Miss Sophie know they're coming. She can warn all the mothers to keep a close eye on their daughters." *Not funny at all, Preach.* Why did he constantly say the wrong thing? He'd never been such a dunderhead.

If Isabelle took what he said as an insult, she wasn't letting on. Preach gripped her elbow and guided her toward the cobblestone path crossing the lawn to the front door.

"I haven't been back," she said.

"To church, you mean?"

"Not since," a rosy flush peeked above her collar, "well, you know. I couldn't bring myself to face them, the folks I'd known my whole life. I felt like I'd let more than my family down. I'd let the whole church down, too."

He'd seen enough of it. Some decisions changed the entire course of a person's life. The people of Stony Creek didn't know Isabelle's secret, though. "Nobody knows you here. You'll be fine."

"I'd like to think so, but I just don't have that much faith in people anymore."

~

*T*he church lawn was filled with people. Isabelle's gaze drew to the statuesque woman crossing toward them. As she grew closer, the woman's catlike blue eyes, accented by long, curled lashes, fixed on Preach, and her generous lips, tinted a soft plum, turned up in a bright smile. She touched her fingers to the edge of a crisp straw boater hat wrapped with a single, grosgrain ribbon the exact light pink of her dress.

The gesture reeked of a reprimand, and Isabelle's cheeks

warmed under the wide brim of her old felt hat. Mother had tried to convince her to bring her own boater at the last minute and she had refused by saying they were only for the summer season and she wouldn't need anything stylish if she was hidden away.

Isabelle scanned the church lawn. All the young women sported boaters, although none as elegantly as the woman towering before her.

Preach dropped Isabelle's elbow as though it were on fire and stepped forward, causing the woman's eyes to widen.

Did the woman have a claim on Preach?

"Dearest, Preach." She slid her hand into his while cupping his elbow with the other.

The woman's dress was exquisite in its simplicity. Sewn of cotton lawn in a delicate pink, the dress had narrow sleeves with velvet cuffs and a blousy bodice pulled into a narrow waist. Stony Creek held more than a flair for decorating.

Isabelle wrapped her arms around her sleeves in an effort to minimize their leg-of-mutton shape. She was as a complete frump in her plain blue calico work dress, even if it looked better than the other two options hanging in her bedroom. The woman's snubbing indicated she knew it, too.

Isabelle twisted to observe Preach's reaction to the woman's lavish greeting. His face bore no expression, but the vein along his jawline beat a fast pulse.

Pulling from the woman's grasp and dropping his arms to his sides, he said, "Miss Thorebourne, how nice to see you."

Of course. This was Phyllis's daughter. She looked nothing like her mother, or her aunt, for that matter, and certainly appeared interested in Stony Creek's newest pastor.

Preach didn't appear overjoyed to see Josephine, however. What was holding him back? Isabelle shifted on her feet, and Preach made room for her to step forward.

"Josephine, I'd like you to meet my friend, Isabelle Franklin."

The description was favorable, more than she deserved, and thrummed in the pit of her stomach.

Josephine dragged her gaze away from Preach's and tossed a stiff smile at Isabelle before returning her gaze back to Preach's. Her fingers fluttered near her mouth. "Have I met your friend before?"

Of course they'd never met, and Josephine knew it. Isabelle wasn't likely to get a puffed head around this woman.

Preach looked at Isabelle and raised an eyebrow. "I don't think so. She's working at the camp as cookee for Lou, her aunt."

"Oh." Josephine's pretty lips pursed in a delicate O, one she'd most likely practiced in the mirror. "Mother mentioned something the other day about Lou hiring her niece." She pulled at a soft curl behind one ear. "She didn't say..."

Preach bent his head forward as though urging Josephine to say more, but her words trailed away.

What had Josephine's mother not said? That Isabelle was a bumpkin who only wore fashions from two seasons ago? Or perhaps Phyllis hadn't mentioned that Isabelle was so thin it was a wonder she could find clothes at all. *Go ahead, Josephine, say what you mean to say.*

"Never mind." Josephine's gaze flitted to Isabelle and back. "Preach, mother and I were wondering if you would honor us with your presence at lunch today." Her chin lifted to present her beautiful face at a fetching angle not many men would resist.

"Thank you for the offer, but I'm not alone."

The other men would be more than willing to escort Isabelle home in the wagon. They'd said as much on the way in. It would be bothersome, but perhaps the trip would satisfy some of their curiosity, and they would leave her alone at the camp. "I can—"

"Please, bring your company," Josephine said. "Mother won't mind."

No one would mind. Isabelle was no competition at all.

"Thank you. The eight of us will be more than happy to accept your invitation."

"Eight?" Josephine squeaked.

Preach couldn't possibly mean to take the men with him. Josephine had the appearance of a woman from a civilized home.

Preach's mouth didn't hold the slightest suggestion of a smile. He hadn't meant the response as a joke, which only made it more amusing. Isabelle compressed her lips to stifle the laughter tumbling in her chest.

"Yes," Preach said. "Isabelle has managed to convince six of the men to join us for the service this morning."

Josephine's flicker of a smile made Preach's words feel vulgar. Why had Isabelle even bothered to attend church?

"They'll be delighted to know you've extended your hospitality. It's not really a crowd for folks used to feeding four growing boys, but I'm sure you already know that."

Josephine's shoulders drooped as though resigning to the idea that a meal spent with Preach would have to be spent with many. "I look forward to it," she said.

Preach nodded. "Please excuse us. I need to speak with Miss Sophie before the service." He stepped back to take Isabelle's elbow again and led her up the pathway to the double doors of the church.

Several paces away, Isabelle spoke under her breath. "Do you think it's wise taking the men with you for lunch? I don't mind returning to the camp with them."

Preach dipped his head before responding. "We both know that's not true. The men are relentless, and if today's lunch engagement doesn't end Josephine's fascination with me, I don't know what will."

So Preach *wasn't* interested in Josephine's attention. Isabelle whispered, "Most men would be flattered if a beautiful young woman like Josephine wanted to spend time with them."

"I guess I'm not most men."

If he could resist a woman like Josephine, he surely was not.

Preach sought out Miss Sophie and asked her if she would keep Isabelle close during the service. After embracing Isabelle in a surprisingly firm hug, Miss Sophie clutched Isabelle's hand and led her to a polished wooden pew in the second row. Other parishioners were filling the pews, and the din of conversation rose around them.

Several minutes later, the heavy clomp of boots and male banter indicated the other loggers had arrived. Preach directed the men to the back pews. His warning to behave themselves carried across the room, causing more than one eyebrow to rise.

At the beginning of the service, Preach towered over the oak pulpit as he led the small congregation in a prayer. After the joint 'amen,' an older gentleman with a stooped back stepped to the pulpit to lead the singing of hymns.

Twenty minutes later, Josephine's mother, Phyllis, dropped the cover over the piano keys with a resounding thump. The final hymn had been a loud, toneless version of Amazing Grace. Did Phyllis play the instrument the same way every Sunday, or had Josephine informed her mother on the extent of the crowd joining them for Sunday dinner? If it was the latter, Phyllis wasn't pleased with Preach's machinations.

Preach returned to the pulpit and asked everyone to open the scriptures to the third chapter of Romans, verse twenty-three. Miss Sophie leafed through the pages of her dog-eared Bible and smoothed the center crease before sliding it halfway onto Isabelle's lap.

There was no need to share the scriptures for that particular verse. Isabelle had memorized it as a child, as had everyone else in the Sunday school. "For all have sinned, and come short of the glory of God."

Had Preach planned to speak on the verse before, or had he chosen the topic of his sermon after Isabelle had agreed to accompany him? If so, the notion burned. Isabelle knew she was a sinner—knowing that fact had never been a problem.

Every stolen peanut from the grocer's bin, every denial of having eaten the missing biscuits—they'd all been met with swift punishment and the writing of lines. Just closing her eyes, she could bring to mind pages and pages of carefully inked repetition of Romans three twenty-three.

But the childhood incidents of wrongdoing didn't begin to compare to the episode with Daniel. Isabelle's stomach tightened into a knot as the familiar gloom played at her feet. The bottomless hole of shame, whose only promise was to swallow her up and send her tumbling away, away from everything she loved—away from God.

Miss Sophie slid her hand under the folds of Isabelle's skirt to press her gnarled fingers around Isabelle's.

Isabelle returned the grip. The pain of Miss Sophie's sharp ring was a distracting sensation. The shame hadn't haunted Isabelle since she'd arrived at the camp, and she'd forgotten the strength of its dread.

Preach's words grew distant as Isabelle focused on remaining calm and convincing herself not to flee down the aisle and out of the doors. It felt like only moments before the congregation was standing for the final hymn.

Isabelle bid Miss Sophie a hasty farewell and turned to retreat outdoors, away from the closeness of the room threatening to make her ill.

"Miss Franklin," Preach called to her back.

Isabelle rotated to face him. Both of his eyebrows were raised in question. What was he hoping? She would give him a positive comment on his sermon? Thank him for reminding her she was a sinner? "Yes?"

"You don't look well. I was wondering if I should take you—"

A perfect opportunity to be excused from lunch. "You're right." Isabelle wouldn't have to witness Josephine or Phyllis pandering to Preach, nor would she have to discuss the topic of Preach's sermon. Isabelle hadn't heard most of it anyway. "I don't feel well. I'm sure Miss Sophie wouldn't mind my companionship while you're at the Thorebourne's."

"Of course not, dear," Miss Sophie said as she brushed the cameo at her collar.

"It will be much quieter," Isabelle added. "You can pick me up when you're finished."

"I don't mind missing the meal. The boys could join the family, and I could take you home."

Home. The word sounded out of place in reference to the camp, but the thought of curling up with a book on her bed for the afternoon was tempting. The innocent expression on Preach's face revealed he didn't fathom the way Josephine and Phyllis would make Isabelle pay for absconding with their prize guest. Isabelle knew better. "You go ahead and enjoy your visit. You can find me at Miss Sophie's when you're done."

"Are you sure?"

"I'll see you later. Miss Sophie, are you ready to leave?" Isabelle looped her arm through the older lady's and accompanied her down the aisle and through the doors to the fresh air of the afternoon.

As Isabelle and Miss Sophie passed the loggers who were milling at the back of the sanctuary, the one Isabelle knew as Snoop followed them down the steps and onto the pathway.

"Could I have a moment, miss?" The upturned corners of his lips as he bowed before them and removed his hat made his gesture appear more ridicule than respect.

Had Isabelle become suspicious of everyone?

"Good afternoon, young man," Miss Sophie said before patting Isabelle's arm. "Isabelle, if you don't mind, I need to ask

Clara Fuller a few questions about our booth in the fair. I'll just be a few minutes, and then we can walk home."

"Of course."

Miss Sophie dashed after a woman dragging a small boy across the grass toward a waiting carriage.

As Snoop chuckled, Isabelle darted a glance at his narrow face. The laughter hadn't traveled as far as his piercing gaze.

"We haven't met yet." He extended his right hand.

"I'm Isabelle Franklin." She placed her gloved hand in Snoop's.

"They call me Snoop." He lifted her hand and pressed his lips to her curled fingers longer than polite society allowed.

Isabelle tugged from his grip. "I've been told."

Another low chuckle rolled from his throat as he brought his gaze to hers—a challenge.

What had given Snoop the notion Isabelle would allow the impudence? Had Preach been talking in the bunkhouse? Surely not. Her story would have been kept in confidence. "I'll bid you good day, sir." Isabelle bunched the skirt of her dress in her fists and turned to follow Miss Sophie.

As she stepped away, Snoop grabbed her elbow and dug his thumb into its crook. Isabelle stilled. His hot breath tingled her ear as he whispered. "Your pastor friend is not as innocent as he makes himself out to be. Ask him about Lavinia."

Isabelle wrenched her arm from his grip, ignoring his rude snort, and started across the lawn to join Miss Sophie.

Miss Sophie's gaze swept over Isabelle's face. "Was that young man bothering you?"

Yes, he had bothered Isabelle, but she wasn't about to tell Miss Sophie. "He's from our camp."

Miss Sophie tilted her head, urging Isabelle to continue.

"He's a bit forward."

"I thought perhaps he was. I've observed him approaching Josephine Thorebourne."

"Josephine?" Preach's Josephine? "I don't imagine Miss Thorebourne was pleased."

"I'm sure I don't know, dear."

CHAPTER 12

*P*reach yanked the wagon to a halt in front of a white two-story three blocks over from the church. The house sprawled across a wide lot, and a narrow veranda with decorative posts ran the length of it.

Will let out a low whistle. "They've got a nice place here. I'm looking forward to a hot meal."

"What are you talking about, Will? We can't complain about how Lou feeds us." Preach jumped from the wagon to tie the horses to the metal ring in the hitching block at the road's edge.

"Ya, but Lou don't look like that."

The other men's heads turned toward the house. Josephine, an apron tied to her narrow waist, stood at the front door waving. Will and Alvin removed their hats and shook their raised palms like a couple of frenzied fools.

"You boys ever seen a woman before?" Preach muttered under his breath.

"If I'd known our hostess was as pretty as that," Snoop said, "I wouldn't have been as reluctant to leave Miss Franklin at the church." He slung a leg over the wagon side. "It's a wonder you didn't mention it, Preach. I just might get used to this church going." He followed the remark with a laugh and a slap to Preach's back.

Preach squeezed the lead rope in his fist. Isabelle's looks could hold their own against Josephine's any day, and Snoop was dreaming if he thought Isabelle would give a man like him even five minutes of her time.

"Quite the conversationalist, *your* Isabelle."

Snoop wouldn't get Preach riled up again. There'd been no sign of Isabelle, or Miss Sophie, when Preach had left the church to drive the boys to the Thorebournes' home. "Sure, Snoop, I believe you had her eating out of the palm of your hand." Hopefully Snoop caught the sarcasm dripping from Preach's words. "I never said she was *my* Isabelle." Nor would she ever be, but the last thing she needed was a man like Snoop anywhere near her.

"You boys hear that?" Snoop said, "Preach says Miss Isabelle is fair game for the rest of us."

Preach should have hit Snoop in the barn when he had the chance.

Perley removed his cap to slick back his shoulder-length brown hair. "Maybe the two of you could leave off competing for every woman within fifty miles of the camp. Give the rest of us a chance, would ya?"

"Ya, and you can start with the woman on the front porch," Will said puffing his chest and dusting his sleeves before strutting down the front walk.

Clearly, bringing the men to Josephine's home had been a poor idea. If Isabelle were here, at least Preach could have shared the afternoon with her. Now, it would be spent with the usual buffoons, only they'd be even more obnoxious as they competed for Josephine's attention.

Preach followed the men to the front door, where Josephine welcomed them in and led them to the front parlor before escaping to the kitchen. Lyman and Logan, Josephine's fifteen-year-old twin brothers, shared a curvy backed divan of material so delicate it looked as if it couldn't survive the rigors of one teenage boy, let alone four. Picture frames of mixed sizes spread on the wall above the boys' heads. The images ranged from family photographs to sketches of hunts to a map of Stony Creek and the surrounding area.

Judging by the quality of the furnishings in the room, the logging business had been good to Mr. Thorebourne. Either that or he was good at keeping up appearances. Perhaps the family's extravagance also explained why Mr. Thorebourne was looking for prepayment on his logs. It wasn't Preach's business to ask him about it though.

Alvin's smirk indicated he was thinking the same thing.

The fact that Mr. Thorebourne owned a rival camp was one of the reasons Preach had never agreed to visit the home before. It wasn't anything personal, but the camps on the mountain didn't tend to mix. It usually led to wild accusations and fierce brawling.

Josephine's father sat in a plump wingback chair by the window reading the paper. He removed his spectacles and placed them on a varnished walnut table before looking up and acknowledging the men's presence. "Welcome," he said. "Preach, why don't you introduce me to your friends."

Preach swallowed to moisten the dryness in his throat. "Mr. Thorebourne"—he nodded to the wide eyed young men —"boys." It was apparent Josephine's brothers weren't accustomed to having their home overrun by a crew of loggers regardless of their father's business. "I'd like you to meet Horace, lead chopper at the camp."

Horace nodded before perching on another wingback opposite Mr. Thorebourne.

"Will's his son. It's Will's first year at the camp, and we're pleased to have him. Alvin's our best teamster. Perley and Ernest both chop for us. And this here is Snoop."

Snoop threw Preach a black look. The slight served Snoop right for his comments about Isabelle earlier.

"Jasper Rice, sir." Snoop stepped toward Josephine's father, his hand extended. "It's a pleasure to meet you, Mr. Thorebourne." Snoop and Mr. Thorebourne shook hands before Snoop made a display of shaking both of the boys' hands and taking a seat.

No one called Snoop by his real name except Lou and only when she was hopping mad. Snoop was making a fool of himself trying to impress Mr. Thorebourne.

Preach's gaze darted around the room, wondering which piece of furniture would hold his bulk before deciding on a sturdy oak-and-leather chair near the twins.

The loggers kept up a steady exchange in response to Mr. Thorebourne's questions while the twins sat quietly, taking it all in, until Josephine appeared at the dining room archway and invited everyone to be seated for lunch.

Hardly possible, but the dining room was even more elaborate than the parlor. A fire snapped and crackled under the polished mantle of a towering mahogany fireplace. Delicate stencils of birds and curlicues swooped beneath the white corner molding on the ceiling.

Preach's mind ran to the second sparrow he'd started carving for Isabelle to replace the one Lou had broken. If he had some time in the evening, he'd have to continue to add to the fine detail of the wings.

Mr. Thorebourne sat at the head of the table across from his wife. The two older boys sat next to their father, and the twins sat on either side of their mother. Josephine took the seat next to the closest twin.

Preach rounded the table and gripped the ornate pressed back chair next to one of Josephine's elder brothers. The boy wasn't his favorite person in the room, but it was better than appearing to be attached to Josephine.

"Preach, why don't you take the seat next to Josephine?" Phyllis crossed her arms like she did when she meant to have her way.

"I'd be happy to sit next to your beautiful daughter, Mrs. Thorebourne," Snoop stepped onto the lush carpet of the dining room.

"Preach, sir"—Phyllis gestured to the empty chair next to Josephine—"if you wouldn't mind."

Snoop's gaze held a warning, but Preach wasn't likely to defy Phyllis Thorebourne in her own home. He rounded the table to the chair Phyllis indicated.

Snoop pressed his lips into a grim line. "Well, I guess I can sit across the table. Makes it easier to see Miss Thorebourne's pretty face."

Several of the men chuckled as they took their seats. Mr. Thorebourne suggested the guests hold hands as he offered up a prayer of thanksgiving. He kept at it long enough to cool the vegetables mounded in bowls on the table. Half the time, Preach didn't know if he was impressed or annoyed by the officious examples of devotion to the Lord he'd witnessed since becoming Stony Creek Chapel's pastor.

He *was* annoyed, however, with Josephine's tight grip. He coughed so he could cover his mouth and break her hold.

At Mr. Thorebourne's rousing *amen,* everyone around the table tucked into the mounded bowls of mashed potatoes, carrots, and creamed peas. They passed a plate layered in thick slices of roast beef and poured pools of gravy from a leaf-patterned pitcher.

"I think you'll find, Preach, my Josephine's beef gravy would be hard to outshine."

"Mother, please." Josephine dropped her chin and glanced sidelong at Preach from under her lashes.

It was delicious gravy, but Preach would have to be under duress to admit as much. *Impress the others, Josephine. There won't be any courting between the two of us.* Preach had all he needed, where? He'd already decided Isabelle couldn't be the woman for him.

Snoop smacked his lips and drew his sleeve across his mouth to remove bits of potato from his mustache before turning to Phyllis. "It's a shame Miss Franklin couldn't be here to join us for this fine meal. You and your daughter put on quite a spread."

Leave it alone, Snoop. Preach extended his foot under the table and kicked the bottom of Snoop's boot

Snoop jutted his chin, and a smirk tugged at the corner of his mouth.

Snoop's look meant there wouldn't be any holding him back from what he meant to say.

"You've met her, haven't you, Miss Franklin, Lou's niece?"

Phyllis removed her fork from her mouth. It tinged as she placed it on the corner of her plate. She plucked the napkin from her lap and gently dabbed her lips. "I met Miss Franklin the other day at my sister May's restaurant when I learned she worked at the camp."

"We just found that out ourselves, Mrs. Thorebourne." Will swallowed the food threatening to spill out of his mouth as he talked. "As you can see by some of our faces, we've been down with hand, foot, and mouth."

"The knowledge has been circulating the town," Mr. Thorebourne said. "I'm assuming you boys are no longer contagious."

Ernie leaned forward to catch Mr. Thorebourne's attention. "No, sir, but we weren't all sick. Preach and Snoop missed out on the experience. The rest of us were sick as dogs for a week, but we've been back in the woods for six days now. Preach cleared us to leave the camp."

You can stop talkin', Ernie. Mr. Thorebourne doesn't need to know all of our business.

"Are you a doctor, Preach?" Mr. Thorebourne asked.

Preach was certain Mr. Thorebourne already knew the

answer to his question. He probably thought he had to put Preach through his paces, find out if he was good enough for his daughter. It would be rude for Preach to tell him not to bother. He wasn't interested. "No, sir, but we had a break-out six years ago at Svedberg's. I was lucky enough to be part of the epidemic. I'm not sure why I missed out this time, but the doc told us then we were safe a week after the blisters stopped forming. I told the boys as much."

"Is Joe still going to be able to make his quota?"

"These boys know how to work hard. We'll meet our contract."

"Mrs. Thorebourne," Snoop said, "you were saying you'd met Miss Franklin, Lou's niece."

Snoop, for the love of—forgive me, Lord.

"I was surprised when I learned Joe had hired her." Mrs. Thorebourne threw Preach a look of warning. "Of course our Josephine doesn't need to hire out her skill in the kitchen."

"I don't know if you've heard," Snoop said, "but the boss didn't know he'd hired an assistant cook—until she was discovered."

Shut up, Snoop.

"Oooooo," Horace howled, "that was something to behold all right, Lou marching into the bunkhouse, wielding her broom, and smacking every limb within hitting distance. It's a miracle she didn't break some of them. She threatened us all within an inch of our lives if we so much as looked at Miss Isabelle."

Phyllis wrinkled her nose as though she'd smelled last week's waste. "Lou marched into the bunkhouse?"

Mrs. Thorebourne's implication didn't sit right. Lou had been in the bunkhouse caring for the men, something they were all grateful for. "Lou's protective of her niece," Preach said. "None of us would deny that."

"Except when it comes to you, Preach," Snoop said.

Will stopped halfway into stuffing a large piece of roast beef in his mouth.

Thorebourne's home wasn't the place to settle the quarrel between Preach and Snoop.

Nor was Preach going to take any more of Josephine's hand warming his leg under the table. He didn't want to be in the Thorebourne home in the first place.

Preach dropped his serviette onto his empty plate. "If you'll excuse me, ma'am"—he nodded at Phyllis and turned toward their host—"Mr. Thorebourne, I promised Miss Sophie I would take a look at her kitchen sink." And he had—two weeks ago. "I thank you for the delicious meal and the fine company. Boys, I'll walk over to the church and pick up the buggy. You can find your way home with the wagon."

"But you haven't had a piece of Josephine's peach cobbler." Phyllis rose from her chair at the end of the table.

Preach forced a smile to his lips. "Thank you both, Mrs. Thorebourne, Josephine. The meal was delicious. I couldn't fit another bite in if I tried."

"Perhaps another time?" Josephine asked.

No, there won't be another time. "I know your mother can make a tasty apple dumpling. I'm certain your cobbler is something to look forward to."

Josephine's smile slipped briefly before she rose from her chair. "I'll see you out."

"Please, there's no need." Preach turned on his heel to leave the dining room before Josephine could accompany him. He wasn't going to give her any more opportunity to accost him.

The screen door whined on its hinges and then snapped closed as Preach left the Thorebourne's home. Snoop could stir up all the trouble he wanted to, although it wouldn't be near the entertainment for him if he couldn't torment Preach.

Preach couldn't deny he deserved some of Snoop's anger. He never should have taken up with Lavinia down at Babby's.

Snoop could carry some of the blame, though. He used to brag in the bunkhouse night after night about his and Lavinia's exploits.

It wasn't as if Lavinia was exclusive. Any man could have her for the right price. Preach thought Snoop would shut up about the woman when he found out Preach and Lavinia had spent the night together. It hadn't worked out that way, though. Instead, Snoop had taken Preach's actions as if they had been a declaration of war.

Preach had apologized to Snoop several times about Lavinia. Preach *was* sorry. It pained him to think he'd thought so little of a woman that it made sense to get back at another man by using her. Lavinia hadn't deserved Preach's disdain. His actions had been more than immoral, they'd been downright mean.

The thought of what he'd done had kept him up for several nights. One of the reasons he had so little resistance to the speaker when he'd stumbled into the tent meeting at the start of break up. Preach still wasn't sure how he'd ended up at the front, on his knees, tears running down his face, but he'd never regretted the decision that followed—the decision to give his pathetic life to the Lord.

Snoop's constant badgering meant Preach couldn't forget the kind of man he'd been. It bothered him to no end, but even if Preach deserved Snoop's hatred, the women around Preach didn't.

Fifteen minutes later Preach knocked on Miss Sophie's front door. One of her tiny hands gripped the cameo at her throat as she opened the polished slab of oak. "Preach, I—we didn't expect you here so soon."

Preach looked over Miss Sophie's head. Isabelle sat in an overstuffed chair balancing a teacup. Red patches blotted her cheeks beneath swollen lids and damp eyes. She tipped the corners of her mouth up in an unconvincing smile.

Preach had hoped bringing Isabelle to town, and to church, would restore a real smile to her face. It hadn't worked.

"Are you ready to leave?" Isabelle set the teacup aside. "I'll grab my things."

"I told Miss Sophie I would look at her sink." The task would give the women a few minutes to finish what he'd interrupted.

"Yes, please," Sophie said. "I think the piping needs to be tightened. There's a steady drip when the sink is filled."

Preach followed Miss Sophie to the kitchen. She pulled aside the skirt under the sink to reveal a tin pail half full of brownish liquid under the lead trap.

"I'll see what I can do." Preach knelt and slid his hand from the base of the sink to the first coupling. It spun on the pipe as several drops fell into the pail. Whoever had crafted Miss Sophie's plumbing didn't tighten the fittings like they should have. Preach would have to take a look in the back shed. Miss Sophie had mentioned it was where her husband had kept a few tools. Even though he'd died years ago, she'd said she hadn't had the heart to dispose of them.

Dust motes speckled the air in the slice of sunlight from the side window of the shed. The building smelled of damp earth and old grease. Preach opened the lid of the pine tool chest sitting on a battered table where screwdrivers of mixed sizes lay in neat rows in the top tray. Sophie's husband had loved these tools—surprising for a banker. Lifting the tray, Preach revealed another layer of larger tools and the pipe wrench needed to tighten the coupling.

As Preach let Miss Sophie's back door close, he thought he heard Will's voice in the parlor. He crossed the kitchen only to see Will and Isabelle leaving through the front door.

"Isabelle, wait," he said, stepping into the parlor.

Miss Sophie reached out and tugged the corner of his sleeve. "Let her go, Preach."

"Why is she leaving with the boys?"

"Will said Phyllis couldn't wait to be rid of the rest of them after you left. Josephine gave him this to give to you." She lifted a small paper box from the table. "He didn't think it would last the journey."

"But why is Isabelle leaving with the boys?"

"Will asked, and"—Miss Sophie shrugged—"she's troubled, son."

He and Isabelle had agreed to be friends. Why was she running from him? Preach stared at the box. He would rather eat that than the peach cobbler it most likely held.

CHAPTER 13

Isabelle stepped through the door and shuffled to the side allowing three young women, their heads bent in chatter, to enter the Stony Creek Chapel ahead of her. She missed Kittie, the secrets they spoke in Isabelle's second-story bedroom, the inevitable giggling fits as they prepared for a ball and compared their looks before her gilded mirror. The many things they had shared—before Daniel.

The church pews had been moved to line the exterior walls. Isabelle's heart sped its thumping as she studied the groups of four to five women sitting around tables set in front of the pews. The arrangement left an open area in the center of the room.

Why had Isabelle agreed to attend? The invitation from Josephine to join the Thursday afternoon event had come as a surprise. The boss had relayed the message after the mail run on Tuesday and offered a ride to town with Carl, a logger from "way back" as he put it, who often did errands for Joe. Carl had dropped Isabelle off at the church for a couple of hours while he picked up supplies.

Joe's kindness had left Aunt Lou to do most of the supper

preparations back at the camp. Since the conversation in Joe's office, her aunt had appeared resigned to his decision that Isabelle could remain at Pollitt's Lumber. Under Aunt Lou's tutelage, Isabelle had become quite proficient at the many tasks required each day and they'd cooked and baked their way to an affable companionship. Aunt Lou had been the one to encourage Isabelle to get out of the kitchen for the afternoon and to meet some of the other women in the community.

"Isabelle, I'm so happy to see you decided to join us." Josephine crossed the wood floor toward Isabelle, arms outstretched, a smile of polished even teeth.

Josephine wore a blue silk dress with generous brown bows at the waist and neck and included a delicate braided trim dotted with gemstones. The braid outlined the bodice and trailed down the skirt in two smooth lines. The dress, although beautiful, was more suited to an evening walk on the boardwalk than an afternoon of preparing crafts for the upcoming community fair.

Isabelle closed her eyes as Josephine crushed Isabelle's cheek against the white lace of her placket in a firm hug. The gesture was extreme considering Josephine had barely acknowledged Isabelle's presence at Sunday's service. Perhaps Josephine appreciated Isabelle's withdrawing from the offer to attend lunch at the Thorebourne home with Preach and the others.

The boys had raved about Josephine's cooking on the journey back to the camp. Perley's thorough description of the Thorebournes' impressive residence would explain Josephine's fancy wardrobe but not Preach's reluctance regarding the girl.

Maybe he'd changed his mind about Josephine since Sunday's lunch. Isabelle wouldn't know, she hadn't spoken to Preach since fleeing Miss Sophie's home with Will.

"Come with me." Josephine linked her fingers through Isabelle's.

Miss Sophie popped up from her chair at the nearest table,

where the women were stitching and stuffing pincushions shaped like various birds and animals. "Isabelle, sit with me. I saved you a seat when I heard you were coming."

The small town didn't keep many secrets. "I'd be pleased to, Miss Sophie."

"Nonsense, Miss Isabelle, you already know Miss Sophie. Come with me and meet my friend Iva."

Miss Sophie clutched at the familiar shell cameo at her throat and wrinkled her brow. "We can sit together at tea, dear."

Josephine led Isabelle to a table where four ladies were twisting and knotting narrow ribbons of assorted colors into elaborate hair ornaments. Two completed examples nestled on a length of navy velvet running down the center of the table. One was comprised of pleated and braided ribbon in a dark burgundy with a silver bell at its center, and another was made of knotted grosgrain ribbon in light blue, a yellow pompom at its tip.

Isabelle's skills in the kitchen might be wanting, and her embroidery might be lackluster, but years of doing handicrafts with her mother would come in useful for the afternoon's activities.

"Ladies," Josephine said, "please welcome this afternoon's special guest. I'm sure you will make her feel welcome."

Special guest? Isabelle was only attending to help out and perhaps meet some new friends. Her stomach roiled. "I don't—"

"Iva." Josephine urged her toward the table. "This is Isabelle Franklin."

Iva cocked her head, and a drape of blond ringlets fell over one shoulder. She twitched her delicate, upturned nose before replying. "Nice to meet you, Isabelle. This is my Aunt Rose and my cousin Betty."

The two women greeted Isabelle, and Josephine excused herself to go and see to another table's needs.

Iva nodded to the empty chair next to her own. "Please, take a seat. Ribbon hair ornaments sold like hotcakes at the Eagle Lake bazaar, and we're hoping they will sell the same here on Saturday. Have you made them before?"

Isabelle picked up the blue-and-yellow design from the velvet. A four-pronged comb was stitched to its back. "No, but I've done a lot of handwork with my mother. These are beautiful." They might even replace the boater hat as the church's next fashion accessory.

"I made this one," Iva said, plucking the ornament from Isabelle and returning it to the table. "Pick your ribbon colors, and I'll get you started."

Isabelle chose two tones of brown ribbon from the table, and Iva snipped them to length before giving a brief lesson on the methods of looping and knotting.

The color would go well with Isabelle's best dress. Perhaps she could convince one of the men to drive her to town for the Saturday afternoon fair, and she could purchase her own work in support of the stained glass windows for the church.

She wouldn't ask Preach. She missed him and the letters he no longer sent, but he'd made his opinion known—more than once.

Isabelle snugged several folds of ribbon together before knotting them onto a comb. Betty glanced over and opened her mouth to speak, but Iva threw her a look, and Betty bent her head to her work, nimbly tucking and knotting. The women continued working for fifteen minutes without saying a word.

Isabelle peeked at the next table, where the women were crocheting white and ecru lace wide enough to be used as cuffs for a blouse or a dress. One of the women was regaling the others with a story involving bloomers on a clothesline and a billygoat.

If only Isabelle were sitting at that table, or with Miss Sophie. It was hard to make friends if no one talked. "These hair ornaments are so pretty. How did you come up with the designs?"

Iva didn't lift her head as she responded. "We found patterns in the Ladies Home Journal, most likely the same ones used by the ladies in Eagle Lake."

"And the lace patterns at the next table?"

Iva huffed and dropped her ornament to her lap. "The same. The Ladies Home Journal."

"My mother receives the journal every month and reads it from cover to cover," Isabelle said.

"What civilized home doesn't?" Iva tugged on a knot before picking up the scissors and deftly snipping a thread.

Why was Iva so hostile? Josephine didn't blame Isabelle for last Sunday's luncheon debacle. Rightly so, the blame was all Preach's.

Isabelle continued silently knotting and twisting ribbon with the other women until ten finished ornaments rested on the strip of velvet lining the center of the table.

As Isabelle kneaded her fingers to release some of the cramping, Josephine strode to the center of the room and clapped twice. "Ladies, it's time for us to break for tea. I'm so glad to hear your merry chatter as you prepare items for the church's booth at Saturday's fair. The new windows will be a wonderful feature in our sanctuary."

Josephine had not returned to Isabelle's table, where there had been no chatter at all, let alone merry chatter.

"Ladies," Josephine added, make a circle with your chairs in the center of the room. Mother and I have made some delightful cookies for our tea time."

Isabelle excused herself from the table and slid into the chair next to Miss Sophie's. Fine china teacups were placed on one of the tables, decorated sugar cookies, ginger cookies, and cinnamon jumbles rested on delicately flowered plates.

"Josephine and her mother are such amazing cooks," Isabelle whispered in Miss Sophie's ear.

"Phyllis and her sister have fed the community for years," Miss Sophie said. "I've never heard that Josephine took after Phyllis."

"The boys from the camp said they couldn't get enough of her beef gravy on Sunday and her peach cobbler was delicious."

"I agree, the cobbler *was* delicious."

"How did you—?"

"Preach said he wasn't hungry. He gave his portion of the cobbler to me. I ate it over two days, the piece was so large."

Preach hadn't been hungry? "Was Preach feeling all right, Miss Sophie?"

Miss Sophie placed her hand over Isabelle's. "I'm not sure, dear."

Josephine clapped again to silence the women and then tucked a stray lock of hair behind an ear. "I'd like to thank you all for coming. You've made many beautiful items for Saturday's fair. We hope our booth will be our best sale to date."

The women clapped their agreement.

"Those of you who can are welcome to stay after tea and continue working on your projects. As you know, the tradition for our tea time dictates the newest member of our community pours the tea."

Isabelle's glance bounced around the room from one knowing set of eyes to another. Josephine hadn't given Isabelle any idea she would be the focus of attention. A burn crept up her ears. Her look darted to the table, where twenty cups awaited filling. Her stomach pitched. How difficult could it be? It was only pouring tea.

"Ladies, I'd like to introduce Isabelle Franklin, Lou Franklin's niece."

More polite clapping followed from the ladies in the room.

Miss Sophie encouraged Isabelle with a smile. She pushed

her chair back and rose to join Josephine and Phyllis at the tea table.

As Josephine slipped one arm around Isabelle's back and tucked her other hand in the crook of Isabelle's elbow she spoke, "Please tell the ladies a little about yourself."

Isabelle looked at the eager faces waiting for her to share. The walls pushed in. She drew a slow breath to calm her racing nerves. "I...well..."

Josephine gave Isabelle a light squeeze. "Let's start with where you're from."

Calm down Isabelle. These women won't hurt you. "I live in Seattle. I've come up to Stony Creek to help my aunt as an assistant cook at Pollitt's Lumber." Facts all the women in the room would know since Isabelle's introduction to Phyllis in May's restaurant. Why Isabelle was at the camp was not going to be announced.

Josephine scrunched her shoulders and leaned in. "Aren't you leaving out the most important part?"

What was Josephine alluding to? "Um, I'm not sure—"

"You're to be married!" Josephine released Isabelle's shoulders and clapped. The other ladies joined her.

Did Isabelle's ears just hear what she thought they did? "I believe there's been a mistake."

The room hushed, and the women stared at Isabelle. Her hands began to quake.

"Don't be reticent," Josephine said. "You can tell us."

"I assure you, I am not betrothed."

Miss Sophie stood and walked over to the tea table. "I believe we have a bit of a muddle. Ladies, shall we have our tea? Isabelle, I'll help you pour." She lifted one of the china teapots and handed it to Isabelle before taking another and pouring a steaming serving into the nearest cup. The woody scent of Orange Pekoe drifted through the room.

Josephine cleared her throat and raised her voice to be heard above the ladies who had resumed conversing with one another. "There's no need to be secretive. Rumor has it your intended is coming to Stony Creek for a visit."

The teapot wobbled. Isabelle set it down on the table. "My intended?"

Josephine tipped her head back and laughed as though Isabelle had said something humorous. "Daniel and your father should arrive this evening."

Daniel was coming to Stony Creek? Why? Isabelle hadn't replied to her father's telegram. How could that have been construed as acceptance of Daniel's offer of marriage? And how would Josephine know they were coming? For that matter, how did she even know of Daniel's existence? Isabelle tried to control the tremor in her voice. "Josephine, what makes you think Daniel is coming to Stony Creek?"

Josephine's gaze traveled to Iva's. Iva looked as if she'd swallowed a canary. What had the two of them done?

"Ladies." Miss Sophie's voice filled the room as she poured another cup. "Shall we serve the tea?" Under her breath she said, "Let's discuss this mix-up later, girls."

The tea was served and the plates of cookies passed around as the women visited. Isabelle received several congratulations and questions regarding her upcoming nuptials. She stumbled over her words as she explained there would be no wedding.

As tea time drew to a close, most of the ladies left the church. Only a few stayed behind to continue working on items for the fair. Phyllis and Josephine collected the teacups in oversized enamel basins to take them next door to the parsonage for washing.

Pain had gripped Isabelle's temples and would soon be coursing over the crown of her head. The thought that Daniel might actually be coming to Stony Creek wasn't helping. "Josephine, let me help you wash up."

"Mother's assisting. You're welcome to continue with the others at the craft tables if you like."

"You can answer my questions here"—Isabelle swept out an arm—"or you can answer my questions next door."

Josephine dropped the bin to the table. The teacups rattled, and several heads bobbed up. Josephine stretched a smile across her face before speaking softly. "Your relationship with Daniel and whether you are getting married or not, are no concern of mine."

"I don't have a relationship with Daniel." Nor would she ever again. "But I would like to know how you know about Daniel and why you think he's coming to Stony Creek."

"I don't know anything about Daniel." Josephine picked up the bin and flounced toward the door.

Had Preach mentioned Daniel to Josephine? Everything Isabelle poured out on the way home from town should have been held in confidence. And how had it become so misconstrued that Josephine believed Isabelle and Daniel were getting married? Isabelle trotted after Josephine. "Answer my question."

Miss Sophie, a teapot in her grip, followed Isabelle next door to the stone cottage that had served as the parsonage.

In the narrow kitchen at the end of the front hall, Phyllis was washing teacups in the ceramic sink while Josephine stood by, tight fists by her side. "I won't apologize." Josephine clamped her lips as she noticed Miss Sophie and Isabelle in the hall.

Phyllis turned, tugged a dishtowel from its hook, and dried her hands as she glared at Josephine. "My daughter has something she would like to say to you, Isabelle."

"I do not have anything I would like to say." Josephine's lip curled up into a snarl. Her pleasant demeanor of the afternoon was completely gone. "I think Isabelle is the one who has something to say. She's the one who showed up in Stony Creek pretending to be unattached, leading men astray, while all along she was hiding the fact she was engaged."

"I have done no such thing," Isabelle said. "And furthermore, I am *not* engaged."

Pfft. "I've heard the stories, disappearing for an afternoon with our local pastor, no less."

Was Josephine's anger jealousy over Preach? It was possible, but the accusation sounded as if it had come from Snoop. When and why would Snoop tell Josephine anything?

Isabelle squared her shoulders. She'd taken enough unfounded accusations from envious girls who didn't have their facts straight. "I have not disappeared with any man, let alone the pastor. Why did you say Daniel and my father were coming to Stony Creek this evening?"

Josephine snugged her lips and slipped a defiant expression over her features.

Phyllis shook the tea towel at her daughter. "Josephine, why did you say that?"

"Because it's true."

Isabelle's stomach rolled as she looked at Josephine. The thought of facing Daniel again was making her ill. "How-how do you know?"

Josephine's glance flew to her mother before she spoke. "Your father telegrammed."

"I didn't receive it."

"Iva," Miss Sophie whispered.

Josephine's gaze dropped to the floor as she toed a chunk of broken cookie on the flagstone with her boot.

"Josephine, you didn't." Phyllis's eyes bulged as she gaped at her daughter.

"I don't understand, Miss Sophie," Isabelle said, "What does Iva have to do with this?"

"It's against the law, Josephine." Phyllis gave the tea towel a twist. "You could go to jail."

Miss Sophie turned toward Isabelle and grasped her fingers. "Ellis Wherry, the young man who works at the telegraph office, is courting Iva. The girls must have manipulated him somehow."

"So it's really true? My father is bringing Daniel to Stony Creek, today?"

Josephine's head bobbed once.

Tea surged up and threatened to spill from Isabelle's throat. She couldn't face Daniel. She couldn't ever face Daniel again.

CHAPTER 14

*P*reach slid the third sandwich from his canvas lunch bag and bit off one corner. The bittersweet cranberry jelly Lou had made normally tickled his taste buds, but since Sunday when Isabelle had taken to ignoring him, nothing tasted the way it should.

Horace had commented on Preach's lack of appetite that morning over breakfast shortly before he forked the three sausages growing cold on Preach's plate. Normally, a man stealing his food would've caused an invite for a wrestle outside. Preach couldn't have cared less about what was on his plate, though, and Horace knew it. Most likely that would explain the gap toothed grin he proffered before stuffing all three sausages in his mouth at once.

How could Preach eat or sleep when thoughts of Isabelle swirled in his mind day and night? Sunday's service should've brought her some consolation, but instead she'd taken it as an insult. He couldn't figure it. Why hadn't she found relief for the guilt she was feeling in the verse we are "justified freely by his grace through the redemption that is in Christ Jesus?" He'd found comfort in the words many a time himself.

He missed Isabelle fiercely. He missed her as if she wasn't just a friend.

"You gonna share some of those thoughts creasin' your brow, Preach?" Snoop kicked at the sole of Preach's boot before tucking into a palm sized molasses cookie.

Against Preach's better judgement, he'd agreed to chop with Snoop for the day. Until Mack was feeling up to working, the men were rotating as Preach's partner. He'd avoided working with Snoop until now, and the man's prying questions were one of the reasons. The fact that Preach didn't like him was the other.

Preach squeezed the bite of sandwich down his throat and took a long sip from the water pail before wiping his mouth on his sleeve and swinging his gaze across to Snoop's. "It's none of your business."

"You hear that, Lewis? I'd call that rude, wouldn't you? I'm just trying to make conversation. The man's hardly said ten words all morning."

Lewis's metal file sped its strokes on a tooth of Preach's and Snoop's crosscut saw. As youngest man in the woods, it was his job to circulate the water pail and sharpen the saws if they needed it. He looked from Snoop to Preach before dropping his chin and muttering under his breath.

"What's that you're saying? You find Preach's rudeness unacceptable, too?" Snoop laughed at his own cunning.

"That's not what I said." Lewis studied the saw as his file skipped to sharpen the next tooth.

"Did you say you're wondering—like me—why someone with so little to say has been put in charge of this whole outfit?"

Was that Snoop's problem? The fact Joe had made Preach foreman when the crew had returned in the fall? Maybe Snoop was done being upset over Lavinia.

Resting the saw against a stump, Lewis straightened. "The

only thing I'm wondering is how the two of you made such a mess of this saw. Have both of you had enough water? If so, I'll be moving on to Perley and Ernie. They're bound to be thirsty by now."

By the work day's end, there would be a tobacco colored scum on the water's surface. Preach was thankful Lewis had arrived at their block by noon. He swallowed another mouthful from the bucket before handing it to the boy.

"Give that here. You've been hoarding water the whole break."

Preach jerked the bucket, and Snoop startled.

"Whoa! You trying to soak me?"

What Preach wouldn't give to pour the rest of the water over Snoop's dark mop. He might have, too, if there hadn't been a witness.

Snoop snatched the pail from Preach and took several gulps.

"You going to leave any for the other guys?" Lewis asked.

Preach grunted. "Snoop's only about Snoop. You should know that by now."

Snoop's gaze snapped to Preach as he handed the pail over to Lewis.

"I'll be taking my leave now." Lewis bent to retrieve his own lunch bag from the felled tree where the men had been sitting to eat their noon meal. "If you two don't manage to kill each other before the days' over, I'll see you back at the camp." Branches cracked beneath Lewis's boots as he disappeared behind a curtain of trees and into the forest.

"You ready to get back to work?" Preach asked.

"Well, I guess we ain't talkin'"

Preach picked up his axe. He was bone tired, and the day was only half spent. If he didn't get Isabelle out of his head, things would only get worse.

He managed to reign in his thoughts and continued chopping until late afternoon when he tromped toward a thirty-six inch diameter pine. Swinging with the short bit from shoulder height, he started the scarf eighteen inches up the coarse trunk. Wood chips flew and settled on his jacket.

"You losing your touch, Preach? What's with the chips?" With a sharp crack, Snoop struck several branches from the last felled tree with the long bit of his axe.

Snoop had been trying to get under Preach's skin since they'd set out that morning. So what if Preach wasn't letting the chunks fly. Several minutes later he'd finished notching one third of the way through the tree.

Snoop stepped over and slid his axe head in the pine's notch. The handle pointed due east. "This where you want it to go? Looks to me like it's going to get hung up on those two old poplars. I don't want any widow makers coming down on my head."

"I was chopping in these woods before you knew what an axe was. Leave it be." For two cents Preach would knock Snoop on his head and figure out later how to explain it to the rest of them.

"You might have been chopping longer than me, but you ain't any better. The boys have been talking in the bunkhouse." With a tug, Snoop let his axe fall to his side.

"When aren't the boys talking in the bunkhouse?"

"They usually ain't talking about fearing for their lives. Horace said you would have split him in two the other day if he hadn't ducked. Carl says he won't work with you anymore. He's tired of looking over his shoulder to make sure a tree ain't coming his way."

Carl was always looking over his shoulder. Nearing sixty, the man no longer moved as fast as he should. Joe kept him around because the woods were all Carl knew.

Anger bubbled at the bottom of Preach's gut. He'd never put a man in danger. "You're lying, Snoop."

Snoop leaned in, close enough for his foul breath to singe Preach's nostrils, and Preach lurched back.

"I ain't lying. You go ask them yourself. Ever since you been chasing Lou's niece, you ain't had your mind on the job."

More than likely the men were thinking Isabelle was making Preach distracted because that's what Snoop had been telling them. Preach hadn't sensed any discomfort among the men. "Logging the woods has always been dangerous. You know that."

"You threatening me, Preach?"

"Nope, just stating a fact. But whatever's going on, you leave Isabelle out of it."

Snoop's upper lip curled into a sneer. "I don't blame you. That girl's a fine piece of—"

Preach's fist shot out and connected with Snoop's jaw.

Snoop's head snapped back, and he went over.

Preach cursed under his breath. *Sorry, Lord, I let him get to me.* Kneading the fingers of his right hand, he stared at the prone figure of Snoop on the forest floor. A trickle of bright red oozed from the corner of the man's mouth.

A second later, Snoop coughed, spreading flecks of blood across the moss. The air rushed from Preach's lungs. Regardless of his earlier thoughts, he hadn't meant to hit Snoop that hard.

Snoop's eyes blinked open, and Preach extended his hand. Groaning, Snoop reached out and allowed himself to be pulled upright. Wiping the trail of blood from the corner of his mouth, he said, "What did you do that for? You could have broke my teeth."

"I said leave Isabelle out of it. She's got nothing to do with the two of us, and she's the better for it."

Massaging his jaw, Snoop took two steps back. "You told your sweetheart about Lavinia yet?"

Preach feigned a lunge toward Snoop. "You want to be back on the ground? She's not my sweetheart." And she wasn't going to be either. His shenanigans with Lavinia had happened before he'd met the Lord and Isabelle both, although the thought of Isabelle knowing about it gnawed at his belly.

A dark blue shadow collected on Snoop's jaw. He raised an eyebrow before taking a step back. "Then you won't mind that I mentioned our shared acquaintance—I guess that would be the polite term—to Isabelle."

Preach flexed his right hand. "What are you saying?"

"Last Sunday after church. Me and Isabelle had a nice little visit."

That might explain why Isabelle had avoided Preach all week. He reached for the collar of Snoop's jacket and tightened it around his neck. "You had no right." Preach shook Snoop's collar, and the man's eyes brightened in fear.

Raising his palms, Snoop's voice rose. "Look, I didn't tell her nothing. Let me go."

Maybe Preach *should* finish what he started. "Then why did you say you did?"

"Let me go, and I'll tell you."

With a quick push, Preach released Snoop's collar, sending him to his backside beside the notched tree.

Snoop rose from the ground and brushed the puckers of moss from his jacket sleeves. "I didn't think it was fair."

Snoop better be able to explain himself. "Didn't think what was fair?"

"You acting all high and mighty when we both know you're no better than the rest of us. Lavinia wasn't the first woman you—"

"I know my history." Preach wasn't proud of it either. "But I don't get the high and mighty part."

Snoop's guffaw was swallowed up by the dense brush. "You're kidding yourself if you don't. Ever since the start of the season, you've been acting like you don't know what it is to lose yourself in a bottle or partake of the delights in Miss Babby's fine establishment."

The picture of a smoke filled room, men laughing, and women's low cut blouses snuck into Preach's thoughts. His stomach burned. Snoop had no business bringing up Preach's old life. "You know I don't do those things anymore. I'm not sure why you need to remind me I did."

"Cause I think you've forgotten." Snoop snorted. "You used to be just like the rest of us."

Snoop didn't know what he was jawing about. "What makes you think *I* forgot?" Lord knew how the images of his former life haunted him every day.

"It's not just me. You don't think the rest of us figured out your sermon on Sunday was aimed at Isabelle? The poor girl was squirming in her seat."

"What?" Preach rubbed the two day's growth on his chin.

"The whole 'we've all sinned thing.' You didn't need to bludgeon the poor girl. I haven't figured out why her father sent her to the camp yet, but no doubt it's not because she's an innocent."

Preach squeezed his eyebrows together. "My message wasn't pointed at her. You, of all people, know some of the things I've done."

"It sure sounded that way, and Isabelle got your message loud and clear."

Snoop was trying to get him riled up again. "You don't know what you're saying."

Snoop threw his head back and laughed. "Ha. You're the one who doesn't know what they're talking about. I heard them, Isabelle and Lou, conversing Sunday night."

"Doesn't surprise me. You're always nosing in on conversations you're not a part of. You're worse than a small child. What do you think you heard?"

"It wasn't like that. I went to the cook shack to ask Lou for some hot water. I could hear crying. Lou was trying to console Isabelle, who was blubbering on about how everything was her fault. That all she ever did was disappoint people, including you."

"Me? Why would she think—?"

"Why wouldn't she? Why should she be any different from the rest of us? You think you're better than all of us."

Preach tried to swallow. He had belabored the point "all have sinned," but not because of Isabelle. He thought back to several of his sermon points: we are all worthless, wretched beings. If we've broken one law, we've broken them all. We all deserve to die. If she thought he was critiquing her because of her confession she had it all wrong. His gaze found the trail leading back to camp. "I've got to go talk to her."

"We've still got an hour left. Our count will be down."

Preach grabbed his lunch bag and swung his axe over his shoulder. "Our numbers are already higher than the rest of your week. You do what you want, I'm going back to the camp."

Preach threw his last words to Snoop over his shoulder. "You can thank yourself for my leaving."

Half an hour later, Snoop's words still gnawed at Preach's conscience. It was no wonder the girl hadn't talked to him since Sunday. If what Snoop said was true, Isabelle must have felt betrayed. He'd invited her to church, coerced her even, only to condemn her from the pulpit. He could kick himself for not seeing it.

The path opened to the camp's clearing. Preach headed for the bunkhouse to deposit his axe before finding Isabelle and trying to straighten out the whole mess. Snoop was right. She shouldn't have to suffer because of his ignorance.

"What are you doing back here?" Joe Pollitt stood outside the office door, a sheaf of papers clutched in his fist.

Showing up at camp early was a cardinal sin if somebody

wasn't half dead. Preach cleared his throat. "I came back to talk to Isabelle."

Joe shook his head. "I guess that girl's leaving. I told her she wasn't to encourage anyone, although I'm surprised it's you."

"She didn't encourage me. I've got to clear something up is all."

"Seeing as you're here, I need to talk to you." The office door squeaked on its hinges as Joe stepped over the threshold and motioned for Preach to follow him.

"But I got to—"

"Inside."

It appeared Joe was in no mood for argument. Preach stepped into the office and took the chair next to the wall. Joe sat at the desk and lifted a paper from its surface. A stack of twenty dollar bills lay next to a cotton bag.

"I've been making up the month's paychecks and thought I'd do an inventory on the supply box. According to your records, we're short two pairs of pants and five blankets. You forget to record some of the boy's purchases?"

Preach had forgotten to ask Joe about the blankets. Apparently Joe wasn't the cause of the shortage. Preach could look into it later though, Isabelle was more important.

"Maybe you've got another tally somewhere, and you neglected to write it down on the record." Joe tapped on the desk waiting for Preach's reply.

Stealing had been a problem last season, too, and Joe had run off the previous foreman because of it. "No. I write it all down when I hand the stuff over."

"You keep the box locked, don't you?"

Preach did, but it was easy enough to borrow the key if a man wanted to be sneaky. He hadn't seen anyone with a new blanket in the bunkhouse lately. The goods were probably being sold at another camp.

Leaning forward, Joe rested his elbows on the desk and clasped his fists. "You'll find out who stole the merchandise or you'll leave."

Preach didn't want to leave Joe's camp. He'd worked with this crew for six years, and, other than Snoop, they were a fine bunch. Isabelle was at the camp, too. The thought of not being able to see her wrenched his innards, even if it shouldn't. "Don't you think that's harsh?" Preach flicked out his chin. "I'll find out who's doing it. If I don't, you can take what's missing out of my pay."

"Look, I made you foreman because I thought you could handle the men. Making sure there isn't a thief in their midst is part of that. You came back this season different, Preach, and I'm depending on you."

Preach would tie the key around his neck if that's what it took to prevent anymore thieving, but how would he figure out who had already helped themselves to the inventory? He'd scoured the whole camp and the surrounding bush last week for a crate of raisins Lou had claimed went missing. She had suspected the woods might hold a barrel of the fruit well on its way to becoming moonshine but Preach's search hadn't turned one up. Somebody in the camp was thieving and it was up to him to solve the problem. "I understand. Can I go and find Isabelle, now?"

"I'm only letting the girl stay because she said she has nowhere to go. But that won't be my problem. If you come back early again, she's gone."

"Agreed, am I excused?"

Joe leaned back in his chair. "She's not here."

"Where is she?"

"She and Carl left for town after lunch. Carl was doing the supply run, and the girl was helping out at the church."

The fundraiser for the new windows—Josephine had

babbled on about it over Sunday's dinner. "You mind if I take one of the horses?"

"You're puttin' in a lot of effort just to clear something up."

So what if he was, Isabelle deserved it. She deserved a whole lot. "You going to answer my question?"

"Pick up some more blankets while you're there."

CHAPTER 15

*I*sabelle's gaze stayed glued to the muted colors of the tapestry she'd missed seeing on her other visits to Miss Sophie's home. The scene, hanging above the horsehair settee, shot spasms up her backbone. A young man, blond hair unfashionably long, extended his gloved palm to a woman ascending the steps of a carriage parked on a wide drive. Lush trees, moonlight reflecting off their leaves, and twisted trunks marred by shadows bordered the image. The woman's head tilted at a strange angle.

Run. Don't take his hand. You can't trust him.

"Isabelle?" Miss Sophie said. "Are you sure you're well? Here's some more tea."

If she had to drink. One. More. Cup. Isabelle swallowed to tame the nausea building in her stomach.

Wrinkling her brow, Miss Sophie pointed toward the brocade sofa. "I think you should sit down." She rushed over to fluff the red pillows nesting in the corner before gesturing for Isabelle to take a seat. "You're very pale. Has the willow bark helped your headache yet?"

Nothing would help. Nobody could protect her. "I'm sorry, but I don't think I can stay." Isabelle thrust the saucer back into Miss Sophie's knobby fingers and spun toward the door. Where could she run? To the camp? Father and Daniel might arrive within hours. To the church? It wouldn't be long before Josephine inflicted more of her cruelty

"Of course, dear, you've had a trying afternoon, perhaps I can help."

Help? A single tear escaped Isabelle's eye and slid down her cheek. *She* was beyond help. Nor would her warning to the woman in the tapestry have any effect. The repulsive scoundrel would have his way with the unsuspecting lady, and there was nothing she could do about it. Her hands shook in their familiar tremor. She missed Preach's calming influence. If he hadn't been so self-righteous, they still might be friends.

"Isabelle, I really must insist you sit down." Miss Sophie placed the saucer on a side table and gripped Isabelle's quaking shoulders before turning them and pressing her to sit down on the settee under the tapestry. Miss Sophie's eyes were full of concern as she hovered from the matching chair.

Isabelle stared at the clenched fists in her lap. When would she be free from Daniel's grip on her thoughts? She could not bear seeing him.

Not only was he coming to Stony Creek, but he was bold enough to arrive with her father. The father who didn't know the real reason Isabelle hid away in her room for five months, the reason she hadn't eaten, hadn't slept. The reason fear was now her constant companion.

The reason she would never be a fit mate for a decent man.

Perhaps their arrival together could serve a purpose. Isabelle shifted on the settee. Daniel deserved to witness Father's face when she told him what Daniel had really done. Today, she could break her silence. Daniel's future at Franklin, Owen, and

Sons would be over. If word got out, his reputation would be irreparable elsewhere, too. Daniel had made a grave mistake in convincing her father to bring him to Stony Creek.

"Isabelle, dear, tell me about Daniel."

"Pardon?" Had Miss Sophie read her thoughts?

"Josephine seems to think you have a fiancé named Daniel."

Isabelle's stomach lurched. "I can assure you, Miss Sophie, Daniel and I will not be getting married."

Miss Sophie's narrow eyebrows pulled into a vee. "Why is Daniel coming to Stony Creek with your father then?"

A good question, as bravery didn't suit Daniel. "I'm not certain. Daniel and I only courted briefly." The words sounded too polite considering how the relationship had ended.

Miss Sophie patted Isabelle's hand, urging her to continue.

Isabelle picked at a stray thread from the seam on her sleeve. Why had it been so easy to share with Preach? The words had tumbled out, flowed, until the end of Isabelle's story when Preach had looked at her with pity, near disgust, and said the words. The words that had pierced her heart and confirmed what she already knew to be true about herself.

Isabelle swallowed the pain of Preach's rejection. He had nothing to do with Daniel.

"Perhaps all is not lost, Isabelle, Maybe he's coming in hopes of renewing your relationship."

The man was mad if he thought so. "It's not possible, Miss Sophie, nor will it ever be. We parted in very difficult circumstances."

Miss Sophie's remarks raised a question. Why *was* Daniel coming to Stony Creek? For that matter, why was Isabelle's father driving to the camp when he'd made it clear the week before she was not welcome at home unless she accepted Daniel's proposal. "I really don't understand why Daniel and my father sent a telegram to say they were coming. When I went to

ROCKY MOUNTAIN REDEMPTION

the telegraph office last week, my father replied that I could return *only* if I accepted Daniel's offer of marriage. That will never happen."

Miss Sophie tipped her head and scrunched her nose as she studied Isabelle. "I don't understand, dear."

"My father doesn't know what occurred between Daniel and me. I was so angry at my father's answer, I didn't reply."

"On the day I met you, you didn't mention why you weren't returning to your home."

No, Isabelle hadn't, nor would she have now if not for the afternoon's events at the church. "I'm sorry. I should have explained." Life was much easier when Isabelle hid away in her room. She didn't have to explain anything to anyone.

"I don't know how to say this kindly," Miss Sophie said.

Isabelle deserved it, the chastening for not replying to Father and causing the confusion. She dropped her chin to her chest before speaking in a whisper. "Go ahead, say it." She tensed her back to receive the chiding.

"Dearest Isabelle, don't look so worried. I'm not unhappy with you."

Miss Sophie wasn't angry with her? Isabelle let out a slow breath.

"I've been thinking about this afternoon, and I'm wondering if Josephine and Iva might have done more damage than you know of."

Phyllis had rushed Miss Sophie and Isabelle from the cottage immediately after discovering Josephine's part in the debacle. Phyllis had also promised to do what she could to set the matter straight. "What do you mean?"

"Regarding Daniel."

Josephine's unfounded jealousy over Preach had caused her a slip in judgment. What would that have to do with Daniel? "I don't understand."

"There was an incident in town about three months ago. It caused quite a stir." Miss Sophie turned to look out the parlor window.

Isabelle's gaze followed Miss Sophie's. A bit of crumpled newspaper leapt in the wind and rolled across the empty train platform. The grandfather clock chimed four.

"One of the local women, a matron really...well...a man showed up at her door unexpectedly with an offer of marriage." Soft pink collected at the throat of Miss Sophie's collar.

"That sounds quite romantic, but how is it related to Josephine and Iva?"

"It would have been romantic, I suppose"—Miss Sophie's voice faltered—"if the situation had been different. The man in question received a telegram advising him the woman in question looked forward to his proposal, so he hastened to Stony Creek to offer his love to her."

"And?"

"The young man—very young man—believed he had received the telegram from the woman with whom he had been corresponding. He and the woman had begun writing after he replied to a personal ad looking for companionship. However, the woman had ceased answering his letters when she discovered the young man's age."

"Why did he receive the telegram then inviting his proposal?"

"That's the mystery. The matron was mortified to find an eighteen-year-old man—boy—on her front step, down on one knee, and holding a red rose."

Isabelle gasped. "Miss Sophie?"

"It wouldn't have been so awful"—Miss Sophie's voice hitched—"if I hadn't lived on Main Street and across from the train station where everyone in town could witness the scene." Miss Sophie looked down and twisted her fingers in the cotton of her periwinkle skirt.

"Miss Sophie, I'm so sorry. How could someone be so cruel?"

"It was a trying time. I think perhaps it was the Lord's way of correcting a foolish old woman's desire." Miss Sophie smoothed the lap of her dress before continuing. "However, I would have rather He corrected me privately."

"How can you believe it was the Lord's doing?"

"I really don't know, but now I suspect Iva and Josephine may have had something to do with it. Your circumstances today appear oddly similar."

She tipped her head as she studied her friend. "What are you thinking?"

"Preventing the delivery of the telegram informing you of the men's arrival today is indicting enough, but I suspect the girls may have also replied without your knowledge. In my instance, I telegrammed the besotted young man to inform him we would never be married and that our correspondence was over. If he had received *my* telegram, he wouldn't have shown up at my door."

"You can't blame yourself. If Josephine and Iva are responsible, they should be held to account."

Miss Sophie's gaze rose to meet hers. "For both of us."

Isabelle's stomach rolled into a tight ball. "Are you saying you believe Josephine or Iva may have telegrammed my father, and he and Daniel are coming to Stony Creek because they think I have accepted Daniel's proposal?" Isabelle's breath wedged in her chest.

"It's likely."

Josephine *had* appeared confident of her announcement before tea at the church. How had she dared? "What will I do, Miss Sophie? I can't face Daniel. If he thinks I've forgiven him, if he thinks I'll just forget what happened and go ahead and marry him."

Tilting her head to the side, Miss Sophie asked, "Why haven't you forgiven him?"

She closed her eyes as the memory assailed her.

*D*aniel *eyed her with cold scrutiny when he finished having his way with her in the carriage.*

"Tidy yourself. I don't want to arrive at the Allen's with you looking like a guttersnipe. Isabelle's arms trembled—pain coursed through her insides. She crossed her arms over her chest. If only she could disappear into the tufts of the upholstered bench. Or go back in time before she'd gotten into the carriage—before she'd ever met Daniel. How could she have believed he was a man of honor?

"Don't bother looking like a victim." Daniel tossed his head to remove the lock of hair that had pulled from the leather thong at the nape of his neck. "If you'd complied, the whole thing would have gone easier. You might even have enjoyed it." He smirked and slowly slid on his leather gloves.

Isabelle tightened her arms to still their trembling. How could Daniel be so calm? "What will my father think of his golden boy now"—the words caught in her throat and then spilled out—"now that you've done this?" A sob wrenched from her chest. "He will never forgive you."

Daniel leaned forward and gripped Isabelle's chin, pushing her head against the seat back. "He won't have anything to forgive me for, because you won't tell him."

As Daniel's foul breath assaulted Isabelle's nostrils, she twisted her head to break his grip. He laughed before digging his gloved fingers further into the flesh on either side of her jaw. "Let me go," she pleaded.

"I will," he hissed, "but not before we have an understanding. You will not breathe a word of what went on in this carriage to anyone."

If Daniel thought Isabelle would keep his dirty secret, he was mistaken. Even if she tried, her parents would know something had happened the minute they saw her. "Let me go." She pushed at Daniel's chest.

He pressed closer. "Pardon, I didn't hear you."

The pain was shifting to her lower back as her stomach rolled and threatened to spill its contents. "Let me go," she ground out again.

"Do I have your word?" Daniel's bleak eyes, shot with red streaks, bore into hers.

"Why wouldn't I tell my parents? They deserve to know what kind of a man you are and what you've done."

"Are you certain? How would you explain your presence in the carriage without the delightful Kittie as a chaperone?"

Shame burned its way across Isabelle's chest. Why had she let Daniel convince her to get into the carriage?

"Perhaps we could discuss the time you chose to meet me along the river for a picnic—alone."

It was true. Isabelle had betrayed her parents' trust by letting them believe she was with Kittie and her brothers.

"Or they might be interested to hear about our luncheon at the Diller last week."

Isabelle had excused herself from making calls with Mother by claiming she had a headache only to sneak out and meet Daniel downtown.

"Stop." Finally twisting from Daniel's grip, Isabelle buried her face in her hands. She was a liar. She'd deceived her parents for weeks. Why would they believe anything she told them?

"You've been teasing me for months."

It wasn't true. The attention Daniel had given Isabelle had made her feel special, but she never imagined he would take the liberty to—

"All those coy looks from under your lashes, the stolen kisses in the gazebo on the back lawn, I knew what they really meant. We'll be married before the summer's end. There's no need to tell anyone. My sweet."

The endearment sounded more like a curse and curdled the contents of Isabelle's stomach. She would never marry a monster like Daniel. Isabelle dove for the carriage door.

Daniel leaped off the bench and grabbed a fistful of her hair. Her head snapped back. Her boots scraped on the carriage floor, and pain sliced across her scalp as he pulled her into his lap. Her skin crawled at the contact.

Wrapping his arms around her waist, he spat into her ear. "We'll arrive at the Allen's in a few minutes. As I said, make yourself presentable."

She opened her eyes, forced herself to take in her surroundings. Not the carriage. Miss Sophie's parlor. She was safe. "I don't think you'll understand, but trust me, what Daniel did was unforgivable." Nor did Isabelle want to tell Miss Sophie about the shame that scorched its way through the knowledge of Isabelle's part in the incident.

"Nothing is unforgivable, Isabelle. I may not understand, but I think you should tell me regardless. Then we can figure out what to do when Daniel and your father arrive."

Why not? It wasn't as if it mattered. As Preach had said, she was not an innocent, a woman who would never make a fitting wife for a pastor.

Miss Sophie sat quietly as Isabelle recounted Daniel's arrival in Seattle and his subsequent wooing. Her face paled at the telling of his attack in the carriage the night of the May Ball.

"My dear, I'm sorry." Tears dripped from Miss Sophie's eyes as she patted Isabelle's arm. "It must have been so difficult for you."

Isabelle's chest warmed at the understanding in Miss Sophie's voice, even if Isabelle didn't deserve it. She dropped her head. "I shouldn't have encouraged his attention."

"Dearest, whether you encouraged him or not, Daniel should never have—"

"But I met him alone without a chaperone several times. I lied to my parents. I had been teasing him for months."

Miss Sophie dropped her voice to a whisper. "So you think it's your fault Daniel raped you?"

Isabelle gasped. "Raped me? That's a vicious word, Miss Sophie. I wouldn't consider what Daniel did to me rape."

"Because you invited his attack?"

"I did not invite his attack!" Miss Sophie was mistaken. "I would do anything to take the evening back." How many times had Isabelle reimagined the May Dance when she did not ascend the steps into the carriage with Daniel?

"Then why do you think you're responsible for Daniel's behavior?"

"I shouldn't have gone without Kittie. I knew it was against my parents' wishes."

"That's true, but why are you responsible for what Daniel did?"

"I don't think he meant to do it. He had too much to drink before he arrived."

"So that night, the carriage went directly to the Allen's home?"

"No." She shook her head, remembering. "When we left, we drove toward the lake."

"Why do you think that was?"

The Allens lived only a ten-minute drive from Isabelle's home. Why had Daniel and Isabelle headed in the opposite direction? "You think Daniel *planned* to seduce me?"

"Rape, dear." Miss Sophie clutched Isabelle's forearm. "Daniel raped you."

Raped? Was that why Isabelle's heart had never stopped hurting? Why she hadn't been able to sleep the night through since it had happened? The tremors, the headaches, the nausea, they weren't, as the doctor implied, because she was hysterical?

Isabelle pressed her palms to her eyes and leaned forward. Daniel's attack wasn't her fault. Had it really never been her fault?

Miss Sophie rubbed Isabelle's back as the tears coursed down her palms and spilled onto her lap.

"As I said, nothing is unforgivable, Isabelle. I suspect, my dear, the situation with Daniel will provide plenty of opportunity to offer forgiveness. The same forgiveness Jesus extends to each one of us."

CHAPTER 16

*P*reach ran the stairs to Miss Sophie's front door two at a time. The sooner he cleared up the misunderstanding in Isabelle's thinking, the better. Josephine had waylaid him at the church, showing him the gewgaws she and the other ladies had made during the afternoon. After he'd asked about Isabelle for the third time, her cheeks had colored, and she'd admitted Isabelle and Miss Sophie had left a half hour earlier.

The glow of a lantern peeked through the front drapes. Miss Sophie was home. Hopefully Isabelle was here, too. He rapped on the door. A few moments later, heels clicked across the floor, and the door cracked open.

"Preach," Miss Sophie said, "I wasn't expecting you. What brings you to town during the week?"

"Is Isa—"

"I've been meaning to ask you if you moved Reuben's tool chest. I couldn't find it in the shed yesterday when I needed a hammer to hang a picture."

"No, I left it on the table where it was."

"Are you sure? I haven't seen it since you used it."

So the thief or thieves had moved on from the camp to

LISA J. FLICKINGER

defenseless widows. How low would they stoop? Preach would ask around in town. Maybe somebody will have noticed something unusual. "I'm sure, but I can take a look if you like. Miss Sophie, is Isabelle—I mean Miss Franklin— here? I need to talk to her. Josephine said the two of you left the church together."

"We did, and she is." Miss Sophie looked over her shoulder. "However, Isabelle is indisposed right now. I'm sorry, if you could come back later, that would be better." The door opening narrowed.

Preach extended his palm to keep the door from closing. "Is something wrong? Where's Isabelle?"

"She's here. She's simply not of a mind to speak—"

"Miss Sophie, please. It's important that I talk to her. I've caused an awful misunderstanding. Would you ask her if I might—?"

"If you might what?" Isabelle's voice rasped.

Was she ill?

Miss Sophie turned from the crack in the door. "Isabelle, I don't think you're in any condition to speak with Preach."

"Unfortunately, I have nothing to hide from him."

Miss Sophie let the door fall open, and Preach stepped inside. Isabelle stood by the dining table. Bloodshot eyes and blotched cheeks, she'd been crying again. Was he the cause of it? If it would do any good, he would lay a whoopin' on his own self.

Isabelle made no attempt to smile as she stared at him through wet lashes. "What misunderstanding did you wish to speak to me about, Mr. Bailey? Please make it quick, though. I can assure you, I am not up to listening to another sermon."

Snoop had been right. Isabelle felt chastised by Sunday's message. If only Preach could wrap his arms around her tiny frame and hold her. He would kiss every tear as it rolled down her cheek. He banished the intrusion to his thoughts. As much as it might be necessary, remaining *just friends* with Isabelle was proving harder than he thought it would be.

Isabelle's shoulders jerked as a long steam whistle split the air. Two short blasts followed.

Her gaze sought Miss Sophie's, her eyes wide.

"It's not the train whistle," Sophie said.

Preach reached for the door knob. "Someone's hurt. The whistle's from our camp. I'm sorry, but I can't talk now. I have to get back."

If he hadn't left to speak with Isabelle, he would have been at the camp to help. As it was, he was six miles away. Any injury in the bush meant a man was miles from the nearest doctor. It could mean his life.

"I'll come with you." Isabelle sprinted to the door and tugged a shawl from a hook on the wall.

"You should stay here, I'll be working the horse into a lather as it is."

"Isabelle, you should stay with me," Miss Sophie said.

Isabelle curved her hand around Preach's forearm. The nerves tingled as warmth spread up his arm and across his chest.

"Please let me go with you. Maybe I can help."

Preach couldn't resist. He wrapped his hand over Isabelle's narrow fingers and pressed them. More warm tingles slid up his bicep. "It'll be rough going. Are you sure?"

Isabelle lifted her chin, chocolate eyes peered into his. "I want to help if I can."

Forty-five minutes of interspersed gallop, fast trot, and Preach running beside the mare, brought Isabelle and him near the camp yard. There'd been no sign of anyone on the trip in, nor had the steam whistle blown again. As they rounded the last corner, Preach's stomach jolted at the scene.

Ten or more men milled near a wagon parked alongside the skidway where piled logs towered over their heads. A ragged length of canvas covered a still form stretched out in the back of the wagon.

That's why the alarm hadn't sounded more than once. There'd been no need. "I'll drop you at the cook shack," he said to Isabelle over his shoulder.

"Go to the men. They'll need you. I'll figure out how to stable the horse."

Preach scanned the group. Snoop was among them—not that he wished the man dead.

Ernie reached out and gripped Will's shoulder. Will's chin dropped to his chest before his back shuddered twice. Was it Horace under the canvas?

"Are you sure?" Preach asked Isabelle.

"I'll be fine."

Preach pulled the reigns and halted the horse. A couple of the men looked over as he descended before urging Isabelle on with the mare. *Lord, give me the words these men need to hear.*

As Preach neared the group, the others stepped aside to allow him next to the wagon. Preach lifted the corner of the tarpaulin. With his mouth open as though he were going to tell a joke, Horace stared up at the cloudless sky. Preach turned to Will. "I'm sorry, son."

Will swiped at an eye with his fist. "It's my fault, Preach. I killed my own pa." A sob wracked Will's chest, and Ernie put his arm around Will's shoulders.

"What happened?"

"It *wasn't* his fault." Snoop tipped his jaw and crossed his arms. "Anybody knows logging the woods has always been dangerous."

For half a cent, Preach would lay Snoop out on the ground again for repeating his words from earlier so glibly, but this wasn't the place, nor the time. Of course Preach had known it wasn't Will's fault. He'd taught the boy himself. Both Will and his pa were careful, more careful than most.

Preach shot Snoop a warning to keep quiet before dropping his voice to a gruff whisper. "What happened, Will?"

"The tree was leaning north, and pa figured we should drop her to the east..."

Ernie snugged his arm around Will's shoulders urging him to continue.

Will looked up, a trail of tears shining on both cheeks. "I was wedging it like he said when it cracked up the stump. It twisted and broke away so fast, he didn't see it coming." A howl escaped Will's throat. "The thing must have thrown him fifteen feet." Will buried his face in the crook of his elbow as his head shook in silent cries.

The whole lot of them knew injury or death was a possibility every time they stepped out of the bunkhouse. Last year they'd lost old man Mackenzie when a log had crushed him. Losing a man didn't seem to get any easier, though. Will would miss his pa something terrible. *Lord what do I say?*

Preach cupped the back of Will's head, and the boy fell against his chest, shoulder's heaving. Several of the men looked away. "He was a good man, your pa."

Will's shoulder's shook before he stepped back and sought Preach's gaze. "I should have known better, Preach. It was a matter of pride dropping that tree where we wanted. It was leaning too far."

"The trees hold their secrets. You know that. Nothing you could have done. Your pa's in a better place, now." Preach's stomach knotted at the lie.

Will brushed at his cheeks as Snoop snorted.

Every one of them knew Horace had no use for religion of any kind. Preach had tried to share his faith with the man on several trips into the bush. Each time, Horace had countered with a joke about pastors and their failings. Alluding to heaven was just something you were supposed to say an occasions like this one—true or not. "Snoop, save your opinions."

"You ought to be more honest, being a pastor and all. There's no way Horace is in heaven, if it even exists."

For the love of—

Ernie stepped forward and pressed his palm against Snoop's chest. "The boy's hurting, Snoop. Leave it alone."

Snoop's gaze darted from one man to another. One by one, they looked away or dropped their gazes to the ground. Snoop blinked several times before stepping back.

"I believe my pa *is* in heaven."

Preach lowered his voice. "We don't have to discuss it now, son. Your pa's body is not even cold."

"It's true, Preach," Will said. "He's been reading that New Testament you gave him."

Preach had given a New Testament to every man in the bunkhouse. But not once had he seen Horace reading the scriptures. Preach had assumed Horace had either thrown the book away or was using the pages to roll the cigarettes he liked to smoke around the fire in the evenings.

"He's been reading it to me at lunch breaks. Told me he was starting to appreciate Jesus. He and his friends weren't living in a bunkhouse, but the quarters were close. Jesus always had patience, even when the others were acting like fools."

Only Horace would have seen Jesus and the disciples that way. "I'm glad to hear he was reading, Will."

Straightening his shoulders, Will stepped away from Preach. "I want you to take pa's funeral."

"You've got a couple of days to think about it. You should wait and hear what your ma wants."

"I know it's what pa would want, and ma would agree. She and the family will make their way to Stony Creek."

Lord, I love these men and consider them part of my flock, as rough as they are, but I don't have a clue about how to perform a funeral. "It would be my privilege, Will."

~

*J*oe gave everyone the rest of the day off, and the men hunkered down in the bunkhouse with a couple of bottles to tell stories about Horace and more than likely repeat some of his choicest jokes. Preach had offered to take Horace to the undertaker in town.

The sun dropped over the crest of Cougar Ridge Mountain long before Preach returned to camp and stabled the horse. Two strange thoroughbreds munched hay in one of the stalls. Someone had company.

Preach's boots crunched on the spruce cones scattered on the path leading to the cook shack as he lifted his hat and swiped across his brow. The day had been hours longer than it should have been.

Preach would miss Horace. The man was good at his job, but he also helped cool the men's tempers with his humor when fights broke out in the bunkhouse. They'd all miss him.

Bone tired or not, Preach needed to talk to Isabelle and clear up her ideas about his sermon. It was more than that, though. He needed to see her sweet face and know that she was safe. Maybe then his nerves would stop their jangling.

Farther down the path, the sound of a man's voice carried through the dining room door. Lou didn't allow the men to visit inside—ever.

Preach smacked his knuckles on the rough sawn wood once before lifting the latch. A young man, his pretty-boy face pulled into a scowl, sat across from Isabelle and an older gentleman with a gray walrus mustache. The buttons of the older man's vest strained to contain his rotund figure.

Isabelle's eyes widened and then a look of relief slid over her features. "Preach, you're back, Ernie said you volunteered to take Horace to the, uhh,"—her glance dashed to the older man —"the undertaker."

"Undertaker?" the older man asked.

Isabelle fiddled with a small curl behind one ear. A nervous habit Preach wouldn't mind soothing if there wasn't an audience. *Lord, help me.* He needed to stop thinking about her that way.

"The camp lost a good man today, Father. He was hit when a tree fell the wrong direction."

Isabelle's father? What was he doing here? Preach glanced at the older man. The dimple in the center of his chin was the only resemblance he had to his daughter. Someone must have filled Isabelle in on how Horace had died. Hopefully, they hadn't shared the extent of Horace's injuries. The undertaker said his entire chest had been caved in.

"Father, I'd like to introduce you to the camp foreman, Charles Bailey, Mr. Bailey, my father, Alexander Franklin"

Preach reached out and took Alexander's smooth fingers in his own. "They call me Preach. Nice to meet you, sir." He threw a glance at the younger man. Surely this wasn't Daniel. It would take a lot of gall to show up at the camp after what he'd done to Isabelle. "I've enjoyed getting to know your daughter."

The young man stood, pushed his shoulders back, and puffed his chest.

Preach couldn't have cared less. If it *was* Daniel, Preach stood half a foot taller and almost twice as wide. He glanced over at Isabelle. Her cheeks were a soft shade of pink.

"You must be Daniel?" Preach wouldn't lie and say it was a pleasure to meet someone who'd caused Isabelle so much trouble.

Daniel nodded.

"The name's Preach."

Daniel stood and stretched out his hand. Preach took it. It wasn't likely that Daniel was pleased to meet Preach either. His grip was weaker than Preach expected. Daniel wouldn't last half an hour with a whip saw.

As though he could read Preach's thoughts, Daniel length-ened his back and crossed his arms over his chest. "Alexander, you led me to believe there would be no interaction between my intended and the men at the camp, yet this man claims to have gotten to know Isabelle."

Preach hadn't just gotten to know her, he'd grown to care for her, too.

"As I just told you, I'm *not* your intended. We are *not* engaged."

Both Daniel and Isabelle's father startled at her outburst before Mr. Franklin's lips worked together as though searching for words. "Lou told me Isabelle would be kept separated from everyone else at the camp."

Daniel leaned across the table. "How did you get to know Preach?"

Her chin trembled. Isabelle was terrified. The knowledge jerked at Preach's chest.

He stepped over and turned Daniel to face him before poking him in the chest. "Miss Franklin would like you to leave."

Daniel's lip curled as he looked up. "How would you know? Miss Franklin and I have matters to discuss that do not concern you, *Preach*."

The way it sailed from Daniel's lips, the name sounded like an insult. Preach pushed the toes of his work boots against the toes of Daniel's shiny dress shoes.

Daniel sucked in a breath.

Yup, the man was a coward. "Whatever you have to say to Miss Franklin concerns me." Preach looked over his shoulder. Isabelle returned his gaze, her eyes were wet with unshed tears. He turned back to Daniel. "As her pastor."

Daniel stepped back and his gaze slunk from Preach's to Isabelle's. "Her pastor?" He guffawed. "Isabelle, would you please inform your *pastor* we need privacy to discuss our upcoming wedding."

They would marry over Preach's dead body.

"Mr. Bailey." Isabelle sniffed.

The sorrow in her words pierced his soul.

"Would you please go to the bunkhouse? The men need you. Daniel, my father, and I have something important to discuss."

The men might need him, but so did she. "I—"

"Please."

Don't send me away. I've made a grave mistake. "Isabelle?"

"Go."

Preach turned and walked into the bite of the October evening. The door slammed behind him. Isabelle should have let him stay. He wanted—no needed—to protect her.

The bunkhouse door burst open, and Lou marched out carrying a large baking tray. Her gray curls bouncing with every step. "It's about time you got back. I figured the men would need something in their stomachs, so I brought them some roast beef sandwiches." She shifted over to one hip. "It's worse than I thought. They're likely to tear the place apart if you don't settle them down. Get in there." She pushed a thumb over her shoulder.

Since when did being foreman mean you were responsible for every half-witted thing the men did? "Let them at it. I didn't take this job to play schoolmarm to a bunch of children disguising themselves as grown men. I'm going to sleep in the storage shed."

"You knew what you were getting into. It's the same thing Georgie did for you. How many times did he come begging food and coffee from me on your account?"

More times than Preach cared to remember. Snoop wasn't the only one reminding him of past misdeeds. His chest gripped like a vise. "What are they doing?" His voice sounded as weary as he felt.

"Will's burning his father's clothing piece by piece in the stove. Perley and Alvin are fighting over Horace's bunk, and several of them are past making any sense."

"Any chance you can brew up some coffee?"

"I'll do that, Preach, you're a good man. I'm not sure I can say the same about the milksop my brother showed up with a few minutes ago."

"I met him."

"Isabelle's face paled like she'd seen a ghost when they walked through the dining room door."

CHAPTER 17

*I*sabelle's stomach clamped down on the knot which had formed the moment Daniel stepped into the dining room with Father. Across from her, Daniel shifted in his chair before slicking back his heavily oiled waves. *Try all you want, you will never compare to a man like Preach.*

"How have you been here at the camp?" He sent her a look that might have been intended as a smile.

Daniel's simpering concern for her welfare wasn't believable. She knew who he really was. She pushed back the memories of Daniel's attack. She needed a clear head to say what she had to say.

"It's been good for me." She looped an arm through Father's.

Father smiled. If only he knew how hurtful it was to look upon the evil man who had caused her so much pain. She should have told Father the truth from the start.

Preach knew, and yet Isabelle had asked him to leave. Why had she done it?

The answer was simple. He only cared for her as a pastor, not as a man cared for the woman he loved—the way she wanted him to care. The knowledge hurt, it burned her heart like a red-hot coal.

Isabelle rose from her chair. She couldn't spend one more minute making small talk with Daniel and Father. "I'll see to the tea." She scurried to the kitchen and filled the kettle, stoked the fire, and returned the dry dishes to their shelves. Anything to avoid returning to Daniel and her father.

Father peeked his head through the door from the dining room. "Come speak with us. Lou said she would serve us when she returned."

Isabelle didn't have the courage to defy her father. She followed him to the dining room and returned to her seat.

Daniel reached across the table. "Dearest, Isabelle."

Her insides twisted at the endearment and she pulled back. How had she ever thought him adorable? "As I've told you many times, I am not your dearest." Nor had he treated her as if she was.

"I must admit, I'm confused. Please give me a few minutes to speak with you alone. I know I've made some errors. We need to talk it over."

"Errors? You consider what you did to me an error?" Isabelle turned toward Father. "I need to tell you something I should have told you months ago." Clasping her hands to still their vibrating, she drew in a slow breath. *Help me, Lord, to speak the words.*

Desperation written on his features, Daniel turned to her father as well. "Sir, if you could give me a few private moments with your daughter, I'm sure we can come to an understanding."

Miss Sophie had given Isabelle an understanding, she didn't need any other. "Father—"

The outside door swung open and Aunt Lou approached them carrying the tray she'd taken to deliver an enormous load of sandwiches she and Isabelle had made for the men in the bunkhouse. "I'm sorry I couldn't feed you earlier. The men are in quite a state, but they should calm down now that Preach is back."

Isabelle needed his calmness. She shouldn't have sent him away.

"I can make you both a plate. There's some leftover roast beef and it won't take me long to fry up some potatoes. I would have been more prepared, but no one mentioned you were coming."

Aunt Lou's look of reprimand was undeserved. Isabelle could have told her that Father and Daniel were coming to the camp, but she'd hoped Miss Sophie was wrong and Josephine hadn't actually sent a telegram. "I'm sorry, Aunt Lou. I didn't know they were arriving."

"Well, you're here now. I'll get the food on."

Daniel chuckled as the door closed behind Aunt Lou. "So shy, my sweet."

The endearment crept up Isabelle's spine, she turned away from Daniel.

His eyes darkened, but he covered his anger with another laugh. "How do you explain the telegram you sent to your father saying you were accepting my proposal? You requested we come and retrieve you."

Josephine's hateful actions were the least of Isabelle's worries right now. "*I* didn't send the telegram."

Both Daniel and Father's mouths gaped.

Daniel recovered his composure first. "Surely, you don't expect us to believe someone accepted a marriage proposal on your behalf." He sniggered.

Even to Isabelle's ears, the suggestion sounded ridiculous. Father and Daniel stared at her waiting for an explanation. She swallowed. "I didn't send the telegram, but I know who did."

"Alexander," Daniel said. "Surely you can understand how much bewilderment your daughter's words have caused me. I truly believe Isabelle and I should discuss the matter between the two of us—alone."

"I will not be alone with you, Daniel."

Father fiddled with the tip of his mustache. "Isabelle, the matter is perhaps best discussed between you and Daniel first." He cleared his throat. "He came here fully expecting to retrieve his intended."

"I didn't send the telegram. A couple of the local girls thought it would be a lark if Daniel showed up expecting to meet with his fiancée. They used the local telegraph office to discover your telegram to me, and then they responded."

"It's against the law." Father's brows lowered. "Why would they do such a thing?"

Jealousy over a man? She wouldn't bring Preach into the discussion. It would only make Daniel angry. She shrugged. "People do all manner of things. I don't know why."

"Have you spoken to the sheriff?" Father asked. "There's a penalty for fabricating telegrams."

"There's a topic of greater concern to me right now." Isabelle wished away the quaking in her limbs.

Daniel rose from his chair. "Isabelle, please, can we discuss this alone?"

Father headed for the kitchen. "I'll give you a few moments. I'm sure there's something I can help Lou with."

"No," Isabelle said to his back.

He stopped in his tracks and turned.

She raised her voice. "I will not speak with Daniel alone."

Daniel's lip curled into a sneer. It was the same look he'd worn after tossing her onto the bench of the carriage that dreadful night.

Isabelle's stomach rolled as the walls of the dining room rushed toward her. She gathered her fists in her lap. "Father, I have something to tell you."

"Do you, Daddy's girl?"

Frowning, Father looked from Daniel to Isabelle and returned to the table.

"Alexander, perhaps you can convince Isabelle to tell me why she says she didn't send the telegram. I've come all this way, I think I'm owed an explanation as to why she's gotten cold feet." Daniel's gaze shifted to Isabelle. "Does it have anything to do with your so-called pastor?"

"I never accepted your proposal," she said. "And Preach has nothing to do with it."

"Your lips may be saying he doesn't, but your eyes are saying he does." Daniel scowled. "I never should have agreed to let you come to the camp. You were too vulnerable."

"Pardon? Father, what does he mean *he* shouldn't have agreed? What decision was it of his whether I came to the camp or not?"

"Oh, so your father has never told you? He consulted me on all the decisions regarding your welfare since you took ill. The visits from the doctor to your home, the fruit cure…"

Isabelle's bowels threatened to empty at the reminder of the prunes Mother had delivered to her room in china serving dishes—as though it would make the mounds of shriveled black lumps more palatable.

Daniel clutched the lapels of his jacket as though he were proud of himself. "The week at the sanitarium was my idea."

Isabelle's pitch rose as she replied. "The week-long bath was *your* idea?" She'd suffered miserably in the cast iron tub wrapped in cotton sheets. Sleep, meals, all had been taken while lying in the tepid water. The doctor had attended periodically to sample her blood, and each time Isabelle had begged him to let her out. The experience had brought her to the brink of the breakdown her parents had feared all along.

She turned back to her father. "I was not ill, I was heartbroken." Exhaustion, pain, and fear had tormented Isabelle for months. It was time for Daniel to acknowledge what he'd done.

Isabelle lifted her chin before she spoke. "Because Daniel raped me."

"Isabelle, please." Daniel's face mottled. "We've yet to discuss the matter." He reached toward Alexander as though imploring him to listen. "Sir, you must understand, your daughter's been unwell. You and I both know how hard we've tried to restore her to health. Her thoughts are jumbled."

"My thoughts are *not* jumbled." Isabelle steeled her spine. "Father, the night of the May ball, Daniel raped me in the carriage."

Father's large mustache quivered. "Raped you? Isabelle, are you certain? Until now, you've never once said Daniel forced you."

"It's not true, Alexander." Daniel said. "Perhaps I was more forward with my love-making than Isabelle was prepared for."

"More forward?" She couldn't keep her voice from rising. "I had bruises for weeks." And the outward damage hardly compared to what Daniel had done to her soul.

Daniel pleaded, "Sir, you have to understand, I was caught up in the passion of the evening. I might have had too much to drink. I would never intend to harm—"

"Father, I'm sorry I never told you the truth. I felt so filthy after he attacked me. I realize now Daniel had planned it all along. That night, he instructed the driver to head toward the lake. The extra distance gave him the time to accomplish..." The words wedged in her voice box and she swiped at her eyes before she ground them out. "The rape."

"I'm telling you," Daniel said, "What she's saying is a lie."

Pulling his heavy eyebrows into a deep furrow, Isabelle's father lifted a palm toward Daniel. "I am speaking to my daughter."

Daniel's voice shook as he replied, "But she's to be my wife."

"I also deceived you and mother many times," Isabelle said. "I schemed to meet Daniel on several occasions without an escort."

"That is the truth, sir. Your daughter is not an innocent."

Father's fist rattled the table. "You will be silent, young man."

"The night of the May ball, Daniel made arrangements for Peter and Caroline to give Kittie a ride to the Allens'. I knew he lied to you, and I still went along with it." She willed her father to believe her next words. "I'm so sorry, I never wanted or expected Daniel to take advantage of me."

Several moments passed and the dazed look in Father's eyes turned to stone. Red patches sprung to his cheeks, his nostrils flared.

Finally, he stood and pointed at Daniel. "Mr. Talbot, you will leave these premises immediately, and I promise you, I will make certain you are prosecuted as harshly as the law allows."

The words washed over Isabelle. Daniel had convinced her that Father wouldn't believe what he had done, but Father did. He believed her! She pressed the heels of her hands into her eyes as tears welled up and threatened to spill down her cheeks.

Daniel's chair clattered to the floor. "You will never prove it. We were alone in the carriage. No one saw anything, and furthermore, she hasn't said a single word about being raped until now. Someone's been putting thoughts in her head."

At Daniel's pause, Isabelle lowered her hands.

Daniel slapped his palms on the table and leaned toward her. "I can guess who it is. It's your burly pastor, isn't it?"

She forced herself to keep her voice from quivering. "Daniel, you know what you did."

Father stood and brought his face within inches of Daniel's. "Leave us," he growled.

"You give me no opportunity to defend myself?"

"Now!" Father's raised voice reverberated off the walls of the oversized dining room.

Daniel stalked to the kitchen door and smacked it before

snarling over his shoulder. "You will never prove it." Retreating through the kitchen, he barked an insult at Aunt Lou before slamming the back door of the cook shack.

Isabelle's father sighed as he slumped into the chair next to Isabelle and wrapped his arm around her. "Why? Why didn't you tell us?"

She stared at the log wall. Her cheeks were on fire. "I was so ashamed. I never should have lied to you and mother. That night…"

"You don't have to tell—"

"I *do*. That night wasn't the first time I'd lied to you. I met Daniel alone for a picnic along the lake once, and the week before the May ball we had lunch at the Diller. I'm sorry. I knew better."

"You did, and it disappoints me to hear you deceived us."

Isabelle's head dropped. "It was my fault Daniel misread my behavior."

Father turned his chair so he was facing Isabelle and leaned forward. He took her chin in his hands and met her eyes. "You are not to blame for what Daniel did."

Isabelle sniffed. Her eyes burned, but she didn't look away from the face of the man who'd defended her all her life. She thought she'd lost his protection, his love. That she would never deserve it again after what had happened.

"It doesn't matter how many times you met him unescorted or where. Daniel led us to believe he cared for you and would protect you—not violate you."

Tears gathered on Isabelle's collar at Father's words.

"We never suspected you needed protection *from* him. When I think about all the times he came to the house to talk to us about your health afterwards. I feel like such a fool."

"You couldn't have known."

"Maybe not, but I should have asked you to explain what happened that night. I should have known better and trusted you. I think perhaps, in some way, I didn't want to hear the truth. I felt it would be too painful. Daniel appeared so genuine in his concern." His eyes narrowed, and a vein throbbed on his forehead. "That lying, scheming... And all along, he was the cause of your suffering."

Isabelle tipped forward and laid her head on Father's chest. "Daniel betrayed all of us."

"How it must have hurt you when I insisted you marry him. Can you forgive me?"

Miss Sophie's words about forgiveness slipped into Isabelle's thoughts. "Of course."

CHAPTER 18

*T*he barn door opened and footsteps crunched on the frozen ground.

"Hold up." Preach struck the light in his lantern and rounded the corner.

His eyes like flapjacks, Daniel reared back. He held a length of looped rope, a dirty bandana peeked from his front pocket.

The man had more in mind than Preach had given him credit for. Since Daniel had galloped past the bunkhouse window and down the road hours ago, Preach had stood watch to ensure the man didn't return.

If it hadn't been for a nicker out in the woods south of the bunkhouse, Preach might have finally gone to bed and missed Daniel as he stumbled, on foot, back to the barn. Preach pointed to the rope. "You're planning to kidnap her?" Preach hadn't figured on any more than Daniel returning with his tail between his legs and begging Isabelle to give him another chance. He was the lowest sort of scoundrel there was.

"*No.*" Shuffling backward, Daniel put his arms akimbo.

"Where's your horse?"

"I don't answer to you."

Preach lifted the lantern and Daniel shied like he'd been hit. "I imagine after Isabelle talked to her father, you were asked to leave. So leave."

"We'd have been fine if it wasn't for you."

"If you think forcing yourself on a woman is fine. You got another think coming. Get out of here before I give you what you deserve."

Preach raised a fist and Daniel dropped the rope before he turned and scrambled toward the trees.

"Don't you come back!" Preach yelled at the retreating shadow.

~

*T*he following night, moonlight shone through the east window of Stony Creek Chapel, illuminating a sliver of the heavy oak pulpit Preach used on Sundays. His gaze trailed the limbs of the tree of life carved on its face.

A lot of good he'd done at the camp today. Joe had ordered the men back to work. Preach and Ernie had taken Will with them. Not because they expected the boy to cut, but because it was better than leaving him to his thoughts back at the bunkhouse.

Will had moaned and cried for nearly half the day, his grief an oozing, open wound. Listening to him, Preach's mood had grown so heavy it was as if his axe weighed three times what it should have. He'd finally snapped at Will and told him to buck up. Will's brows had shot up his forehead, and he'd swiped a trail of snot down his sleeve before stumbling toward a downed log. Muttering something under his breath about Preach being a sorry excuse for a pastor, Ernie had gripped Will's shoulder and told him he could cry all week if he wanted to.

It wasn't like Preach didn't hurt for Will. Preach hurt something terrible. He just didn't know what to do about it. Maybe he *was* a sorry excuse for a pastor. The people of Stony Creek deserved better, someone who knew what they were doing. He'd perform the funeral as he'd promised, even though Will might be having second thoughts. After that, Preach would talk to the elders about finding someone else to lead their flock.

It would also solve the problem of Isabelle. He could no longer ignore his feelings toward her. Although, he'd made such a bumble of their relationship, she might never consider becoming his wife.

Light steps scuffed on the wooden stairs leading to the double doors of the church before the key scraped in the lock. Whoever it was didn't need a key, Preach had left the doors open like he had planned. A woman wearing a cloak with a large hood slipped in and scurried down the aisle.

Preach had arrived two hours before, not only to pray, but also to wait and see if what he anticipated might happen took place. There was no need for anyone else to be at the church, it was close to midnight.

The woman rounded the altar and dipped her head. He heard the soft scraping of coins. The silver plate used for the offering was kept on a shelf under the pulpit. Often, Preach neglected to count the money and turn it over to Harrison Barlow, the church treasurer—another one of Preach's failings. And now this woman was stealing it.

As the woman straightened and retreated from the altar, her face was revealed by the slip of moonlight from the window. Josephine? Preach had figured a woman might be Snoop's motivation for thieving, but he'd not expected it to be this woman. He waited until she was halfway down the aisle before speaking. "Funny time to be changing the flower arrangement."

She gasped, swiveled, and clutched her chest. Several wrinkled dollar bills peaked out between her gloved fingers. "Preach! You've scared me half to death. What are you doing sitting here in the dark?" She secreted the bills within her cloak, and then tossed her head. The dark gray hood fell around her shoulders.

No one would deny the woman was handsome. "I came to pray. Horace passed yesterday."

He was also there to figure out what Snoop was up to, but he wasn't going to mention that. He'd followed Snoop to town after he had snuck out of the bunkhouse when the men settled into their second night of drinking.

"I heard." She took three steps to the pew Preach occupied and sat beside him before reaching for his arm. "I'm sorry for your loss."

The heat of her fingers penetrated through the leather of her gloves and into the wool of his sleeve. No more than six months ago, the company of a beautiful woman and a bottle of The Belt Buckle's finest would have helped Preach forget the pain of losing Horace, too. *Lord, I need to rely on You. You promised to bear my grief and carry my sorrows.*

Preach turned toward Josephine, and her quick breaths pelted his face. "We need to go somewhere and talk."

Her grip tightened as she whispered. "We can talk right here."

Sitting next to Josephine, the heat of her leg pressed against his, felt like a betrayal to Isabelle. Preach twisted his arm to be released from Josephine's grip and took her elbow. "Let's go see your mother."

"My mother? Whatever for?"

"I'll admit she's not my favorite person, either, but she deserves to hear what you've been up to"—and who she'd been up to it with—"like helping yourself to the tithes and offerings of the church folk in the middle of the night. Surely there would have been a better opportunity in daylight to do your thieving." Preach stood and pulled Josephine with him.

"Let me go. You're squeezing too hard."

Preach dropped her elbow, and Josephine smoothed the

front of her cape before lifting her chin. "My mother will not appreciate the interruption to her sleep. You can bring whatever accusations you have against me to her tomorrow."

After you've hightailed it out of here with Snoop. "It's more of a conviction than an accusation. I saw you take the money."

"You can't prove that."

Preach could if he reached into her cloak to find the bills.

As though she heard his thought, Josephine bent her arms at the elbows and placed her hands on her slender hips. When he didn't come any closer, she raised an eyebrow.

Was she amused or disappointed?

"Like I said, we can discuss your accusation with my mother tomorrow." Josephine turned, the arc of her hem brushing across his shins, and stalked down the aisle and through the entry before pushing through the double doors.

Snoop must be waiting outside. Preach shadowed Josephine to the front step. The wagon Preach had found stored in the woods behind the church on his hike from Miss Sophie's last Sunday was parked across the lawn beside the windowless stone shed built when the original church was erected. The shed contained the odd bits needed seasonally by the congregation that were too bulky to store in the church.

So that's where they'd been storing the loot.

Josephine had hitched up her skirts and was running across the grass. Preach gave chase. As they reached the wagon, the door of the shed opened. A lantern's glow revealed Snoop carrying a stack of five red woolen blankets.

Of course. The missing blankets from the supply box.

Snoop's lip turned up in its customary sneer as he observed Josephine and Preach. "Why am I not surprised? Where'd you find him, Josephine?"

Josephine rounded the wagon and stood next to Snoop. "He said he was praying. Although for a moment, I would have said he was tempted to do more than pray on that pew."

Snoop guffawed.

With any luck, Snoop wouldn't see the red scooting up Preach's ears. "What are you doing with those blankets?"

"Like everything else in this wagon, we're hoping they'll give Josephine and me a new start."

"A new start at what?" Preach peered over the edge of the wagon box. It held two barrels, Lou's missing raisins, and a couple of saddles. Along one of the box sides were several stacks of planed planks a nearby sawmill would probably never know were missing. Next to the planks was Miss Sophie's husband's pine tool chest. No surprise there.

Snoop tucked the blankets under the bench at the front before slinging his arm across Josephine's shoulders. She leaned into him, tucking her chin against his chest. "A new start at a life together. I'm tired of working the woods, the long hours, the back-breaking labor, and, thanks to you, no chance to get ahead."

If all the accusations were true, Josephine had made some poor choices, but Preach didn't wish Snoop on any woman. He'd have to keep Snoop talking until he figured out how to prevent the couple from leaving. "I'm not the reason Joe didn't choose you as foreman. He said there was something sneaky about you." Preach jerked his chin toward the stolen goods. "It looks like he wasn't far off the mark."

"You think so, Preach?"

Josephine snickered in a mean-spirited tone that didn't suit her looks. Maybe they were meant for each other.

"What if I told you this wagon here was only a portion of our stake? We've been planning this for some time." Snoop leaned in and kissed Josephine, his lips smacking noisily on hers as she circled his waist with her arms.

Preach looked away. "What do you mean only a portion? Who else have you been stealing from?"

"Let's just say I've been paid well for some of my superior stacks of logs."

The rat. It was worse than Preach had figured.

"My woman here lends a certain amount of credibility to my presentation as a timber business owner.

That's why Alvin had seen someone attempting to measure Pollitt's log piles. Snoop and Josephine must have sent a scaler out to measure Thorebourne's piles so they could get a prepayment. "Alvin mentioned he saw someone scaling one of our piles a few weeks ago."

"That was almost our undoing. The man was lost." Snoop snorted and Josephine covered her mouth. "You know city folk. We'd sent him up to camp four. I don't know how he ended up at Pollitt's."

"Alvin sent the fellow on to Thorebourne's, but now I'm wishing he hadn't." By the time Mr. Thorebourne discovered their treachery, Snoop and Josephine would be long gone. If only Preach had asked Mr. Thorebourne about the scaling the day he'd eaten lunch at their home. Thorebourne's loss would be a hard one to bear. "Are you all right with that, Josephine, you two swindling your own family?"

"That's what made her plan so perfect."

"Josephine's plan?" Preach's gaze snuck to the woman's face. She bore no hint of shame.

"Yup." As Snoop squeezed Josephine's shoulders, a belligerent smile spread across her face. "The woman has a brilliant mind."

Snoop was clearly in love. No one had ever accused Josephine of being brilliant. "How'd you do it?"

"Josephine wasn't a stranger to the buyers. Her dad's taken her on business trips since she was a young girl." Snoop pulled at the lapels of his worn mackinaw. "When we weren't workin' in the summer, I cleaned up and became Mr. Jasper Rice, the new son-in-law, sent to make their acquaintance before fall cutting commenced and to ensure good relations continued between the Valley Mill and the Thorebourne Timber Company."

Perhaps Snoop and Josephine *were* well suited. The two of them were both scoundrels. "Why didn't you just make it legitimate and get married? You would've saved yourself and others a lot of trouble."

Snoop's expression hardened. "I got plans. Like I said, I'm done with the lumber business. We're heading to the coast. We've got a tidy sum to invest in a marine salts company."

"You want to cash in on *sea salt?*"

"Where you been, Preach? They've figured a way to mine sea water for gold using electricity. Not much longer and Josephine, and I will be sitting pretty."

If Snoop thought sea water would make him rich, Preach should have sold him shares in a moose taming company.

Josephine stepped forward and planted her feet. "My father wouldn't allow us to get married."

"Now, sweetie, Preach doesn't need to know all our business."

Ignoring Snoop, Josephine continued. "For some reason, my mother pegged you as the heir of the company. Ever since you were saved, it's been nothing but 'what a fine sermon Preach gave today,' or 'that man's got a real head for management.' She went on and on. With all her talk, she has convinced my father you're the man he needs in the family."

Josephine's story went a long way to explaining Snoop's anger toward Preach, but Preach didn't feel any pity for him. "You never meant any of it, did you? All the chasing me around. I was just a cover for what you and Snoop were up to." Preach hadn't appreciated Josephine's attention, but it smarted to find out she'd only been acting a part.

"You don't know the half of it. I couldn't cook a meal to save myself or anyone else for that matter."

"But I've tasted your cooking."

"You thought you did. No one's ever actually seen me cooking because I don't. Attracting you through your stomach was my mother's idea, and all the food I plied you with was her doing. My mother thought she was doing a fine job, too, until Isabelle came to town. Seeing you around that girl, my mother started to suspect you and I weren't as close as I'd led her to believe. We could have taken the town for more if that girl hadn't shown up."

"Is that why you sent the telegram to Isabelle's father?"

"I needed to do something drastic to convince my mother you were still a son-in-law prospect and allay her suspicions regarding Snoop. How was I to know Isabelle wasn't just playing coy and she actually didn't want to marry Daniel?" Josephine's snort of derision jerked on Preach's nerves.

Isabelle didn't deserve the mess Josephine had thrown her into. When Preach contemplated what Daniel might have put Isabelle through if he'd kidnapped her and forced her to marry him, Preach wanted to throttle Josephine. "You've caused that girl a lot of trouble."

"She's caused me more. When you lost your head over her, Snoop and I had to move up our departure. It's cost us money."

Josephine was exaggerating. "I don't know what you're talking about."

Tipping her head back, she laughed, course laughter that grated on the ears. "Then you're the only one who doesn't. Perley's been taking bets the two of you will be married by Christmas. I would have wagered myself"—leaning toward Preach, Josephine spat out the words—"but I won't be around to collect."

This was a Josephine he'd never met.

"I still don't understand why you care so much about Isabelle," Josephine said. "What does she have that I don't?"

A kind heart, a generous spirit, not even a harsh word for those who had caused her so much grief. Qualities Preach admired on the inside of a woman—not on the outside. The thought filled his heart with an unfamiliar peace. "It doesn't matter."

"I'd like to know."

"Well, I sure don't," Snoop said. "You're twice the woman that girl will ever be."

Not even close, Snoop.

Snoop sent Preach a glare before he focused on Josephine. "Let's you and I get in this wagon and start that new life we've been talking about."

It might get ugly, but Preach could take Snoop down. He had before. More than likely, Josephine would just let the two of them go at it. Her corset wouldn't allow for much more. "You both know I can't let you leave."

"I think you will, Preach."

Metal clinked on metal as Snoop rested a rifle on the wagon box, the barrel pointed at Preach's chest.

He swallowed. The seconds ticked by as sweat gathered at the base of his spine. It had been a while since someone had threatened to kill him. "You shoot me with that, and the whole town will come running."

"It won't matter much to you now, will it?"

"Is that Joe's carbine?"

Snoop dropped his voice to a murmur, "Ya, and it'll make a mess of you."

Keep him talking, Preach. "You don't need to leave like this. If you give all the stuff back and turn the money over to Josephine's father, folks won't even know what you've been up to."

"It's too late for that," Snoop said. "Besides, I've stole before, just not so successfully. I'm not taking any chances I'll go back to jail." Snoop passed the rifle to Josephine. "If he makes a move, shoot him. I'll finish loading the wagon."

The steel in Josephine's look told Preach she'd follow through on Snoop's instructions.

Snoop returned to the wagon three times with items from the shack. He packed four more blankets, a large wooden crate, and several of the church's garden tools before retrieving the rifle from Josephine. "Come around here slow. You can sleep in the shed tonight." Snoop howled with laughter. "We both know you've done worse."

"I'm going to miss you, Snoop," Preach said.

Snoop poked the barrel between Preach's shoulder blades, urging him into the shed. "Ha! About as much as I'll miss you. Josie, the lock's on the box by the door."

Josephine grabbed the lock as Snoop gave Preach one last shove with the barrel of the gun. The shed door closed, plunging Preach into darkness before the padlock scraped on its hasp.

A few moments later, the wheels of the wagon creaked and groaned as the couple drove away. Preach kicked at the base of the thick slab of wood. It didn't budge. Yelling wouldn't help. The church was quarter of a mile from the nearest home. He'd have to wait until morning for rescue.

Reaching to his right, Preach felt his way past two chairs, several rolled canvases, and an old pulpit before finding a wooden manger full of straw. It wouldn't make the most comfortable bed, but as Snoop had reminded Preach, he'd had a lot worse. "I guess I'm borrowing your bed tonight, Jesus."

Preach fluffed the straw in the manger before taking a seat, propping his back against the stone wall, and spreading one of the canvasses to use as a blanket.

No more than six hours' ride, and Josephine and Snoop would reach the coast. They'd probably board a ship after that, find somewhere safe to await their windfall. They'd both played their parts well. The town would be surprised to hear they'd left the way they did.

Preach hadn't seen it coming either until he'd asked a few questions around town. It was Lem, owner of the general store, who'd told Preach about Snoop. The man suffered with insomnia and liked to walk the streets of Stony Creek until he grew tired. He'd seen Snoop come into town driving a wagon several times in the dead of night.

Snugging the canvas under his chin, he tipped his head back and closed his eyes. Isabelle's face rose in his mind like it had every single night since the afternoon he'd met her.

Lord, give Isabelle the comfort I can't give her. She didn't deserve to be misused by Josephine and Snoop. Isabelle's had so much torment in the last year. Lord, help her know how much You love her—how much I love her.

So Perley figured Preach and Isabelle would be married by Christmas. He shifted in the manger, a rough board digging into his spine. Perley wasn't known for long odds.

Hours later, Preach shielded his eyes at the sound of the door opening. Daylight surrounded a shadowed form holding a long shaft. Had Snoop returned to finish him off? Preach's stomach clenched.

"Preach? What are you doing in here?"

He leaned forward before groaning. Sleep hadn't evaded him, but the odd position and the cold from the stone wall had driven pain into every one of his limbs. "Miss Sophie, am I glad to see you." Preach shook his arms to restore the flow of blood. How did you find me?"

Miss Sophie leaned a rake against the chairs and hurried to Preach's side. Wrapping an arm around one of his, she yanked upward. If he didn't hurt so much, Preach would have laughed. Her tiny limbs weren't going to be any use in getting him out of the manger.

Preach attempted to stand, but his feet were numb and wouldn't hold. "Give me a couple of minutes."

Fiddling with the brass button on her wool coat, Miss

Sophie's gaze darted around the piled objects in the shed. "I forgot my best plate in the church on Thursday. I thought I would retrieve it during my morning walk. I noticed the rake leaning against the shed, and I thought I'd put it back. I'm not even sure why we lock it. Everyone in town knows the key is hanging under the eaves."

"It sure works when you want to lock someone in."

Miss Sophie's eyebrows narrowed in a look of worry. "Was someone afraid you might get into trouble, Preach? Was Horace's death too much for you? I know it can be difficult to follow the Lord, but—"

"It was Snoop."

"Snoop put you in here?"

"He had a gun, and he wasn't concerned about the condition of my soul. He and Josephine have been stealing whatever they can lay their hands on, including your husband's tool chest. I knew Snoop was up to something, but I didn't know about Josephine. I caught them both at it around midnight last night."

"Oh, my."

"They'll be at the coast by now. But I imagine you'll find your husband's chest not far down the road with the rest of the loot. I loosened the nut on the back wheel of the wagon when I got to town. It was stashed in the woods, the same place I found it last Sunday on my way to the church from your house. I had a hunch it was the same one Snoop had been using on his late night trips to town. They won't have found the nut in the dark last night."

"Phyllis will be so disappointed."

"I imagine there will be lots of folks who are disappointed." Preach stretched his legs. "I think I can almost feel my legs. Let's go."

CHAPTER 19

*I*sabelle followed one of the paths leading from the cook shack. Her foot scuffed on the step outside Joe's office door. She brought her hand to the back of the plate carrying the fresh oatmeal and raisin cookies to keep them from sliding to her feet. The chill of the October evening brought a shiver to her shoulders—or was it nerves?

According to Aunt Lou, Joe had offered Preach the use of his office during supper, and Preach had taken him up on it to prepare for Horace's funeral. Aunt Lou had insisted Preach deserved Isabelle's good-bye in person, "after all he'd done for her" before she'd pushed Isabelle out the door with the cookies.

Isabelle's heart was torn. Preach *had* come to her rescue. When she thought of Daniel's attempted abduction, her knees quaked. Preach had told her father about the episode to make sure he watched closely over Isabelle.

But Preach had also grieved her heart more than she cared to admit. As far as she was concerned, sneaking off to her home with Father was more palatable than a final good-bye, but Aunt Lou didn't consider Isabelle's promise to leave a note for Preach

192

a fitting end to their friendship. When had Aunt Lou decided Preach's feelings even mattered?

Daniel wouldn't dare show his face in Seattle now that he'd been found out. It was safe for Isabelle to return home and Father had encouraged her to travel with him. Isabelle hadn't spoken to Preach since he'd burst in on her conversation with Daniel and Father. His pained expression when she'd asked him to leave had said she'd hurt him, but he'd hurt her, too. It seemed as if all they did was wear on each other—one more reason not to seek him out.

Isabelle turned from the door. Across the camp yard, Aunt Lou stood by the corner of the cook shack, broom in hand. She wouldn't dare come after Isabelle, would she?

Aunt Lou shooed the air. It wasn't worth finding out. Isabelle's breaths slowed as she turned toward the office door once more and concentrated on the knothole directly below the scrawl of *Pollitt's Lumber* in thick black paint. Preach must be exhausted after last night's escapade.

The supper table, usually silent, had buzzed with the story of Snoop and Josephine absconding with stolen goods and heading for the coast. The men had howled with laughter, when they heard how Preach had the foresight to disable the wagon.

None of the men had appeared surprised that Snoop had taken the opportunity to escape with the pretty girl, but more than one had questioned Josephine's poor choice in men.

If Josephine was truly in love with Snoop, she'd hidden it well. Her overtures in Preach's direction had appeared genuine. Isabelle wasn't sorry Josephine was gone. Isabelle's sympathy, however, extended to Phyllis. The woman had been forthright in her pursuits for her daughter, and she didn't deserve what Josephine had done to the family—no mother did. The men around the table had conjectured the Thorebourne family might lose their business and their beautiful home because of Josephine's selfish actions.

Stop stalling, it won't help. Isabelle swallowed before rapping on the door.

"Yes?"

Preach's voice did sound tired. He didn't need Isabelle bothering him. She should leave the cookies outside the door and return to her packing. She glanced over her shoulder. Aunt Lou still stood sentry at the corner of the cookhouse. Isabelle turned back to the door. "I've brought you some cookies, fresh from the oven, I thought—"

The door slid open, and Preach towered over her, his hair standing in clumps as if he'd tugged at it. His expression softened, the corners of his mouth rose in a smile. "Thank you."

"I was hoping we could talk." There was no reason to tell Preach she was being forced to.

Preach tipped his head. "I've been meaning to talk to you, too. How are you? The whole affair with Daniel must have been overwhelming."

"Thank you for protecting me. My father told me what you did. When I think of what Daniel meant to do..." And how far he might have gone to obtain Isabelle's compliance. "Well, I hate to think about it."

A half-grin creased Preach's face. "Me, too. Look, I don't have a lot of time right now. Can we speak after Horace's funeral? I'm trying to prepare for it"—he swung an arm toward the desk—"and it's harder than I thought. I've only got a couple of words written."

Isabelle's fingers twitched with the desire to reach up and smooth the fine lines at the corners of Preach's eyes. She would miss the serenity found in those deep pools.

Although Isabelle, too, should be exhausted, she pulsed with energy. Two nights before, after Daniel had stormed out of the dining room, she and Father had talked well past midnight. Isabelle had sobbed and shared the vile details of Daniel's attack as her father had held her and told her how much both he and her mother loved her.

Knowing there were no more secrets between Isabelle and her parents had brought her a peacefulness she hadn't experienced since before the May Ball. The anxiety that usually awakened her several times every night appeared to have vanished too. Isabelle had slept the last two nights through, even though she and Aunt Lou were sharing Aunt Lou's single bed.

Isabelle had also been able to read her Bible before meal prep began each morning. There'd been no condemning whispers of *you're a shameful fraud* as she'd opened the pages and drawn strength from Isaiah forty-three that very morning. *Remember ye not the former things, neither consider the things of old. Behold I will do a new thing now it shall spring forth; shall ye not know it? I will even make a way in the wilderness, and rivers in the desert.*

Lord, if anyone needs a way in the wilderness, I do.

Isabelle's good-bye would be short. "I won't take much of your time...pastor."

Her words brought a glow to his eyes. "Thank you for the reminder to consider all my parishioners' requests in their time of need." He pinned her with a forthright gaze. "You do have a need, don't you?"

Isabelle's heart palpitated as heat radiated from her stomach and through her limbs. What was he really asking? She *did* have a need. A need to have the feelings she felt for Preach reciprocated, but that need wasn't going to be met.

Isabelle nibbled her bottom lip between her teeth as he waited for her response.

As the seconds ticked by, he leaned forward and raised his eyebrows.

"I think so." Her voice quivered.

Preach plucked two cookies from the plate and tucked them into his mouth in one bite. As his Adam's apple bobbed, he swung the door open and gestured for Isabelle to enter the office. "I suppose your interruption can't hurt. I have no idea what I should say tomorrow. I hate to disappoint the family, but judging by what I've written so far, whatever I come up with won't be eloquent."

Scraping his boots across the rough sawn boards, he motioned for Isabelle to take the chair against the wall behind the door. After setting the plate on the desk, he picked up two more cookies and shoveled them into his mouth. "Mm. Good. Thank you."

Only a few coals glowed in the narrow fireplace. Isabelle tightened her coat.

"I suppose it is cold in here," Preach said before crossing to the fireplace and adjusting the coals with a wrought iron poker. He plucked three logs from the small wood stack next to the wall. After he laid them on the coals, bright flames snapped along the bark.

"You must be tired after last night's ordeal," Isabelle said.

Preach snorted as the flames highlighted his chiseled features.

Her stomach fluttered again, as if it were filled with moths. Aunt Lou didn't know what she was asking of her niece. Isabelle didn't want to say good-bye.

"I've had better sleeping arrangements, that's for sure." Preach's gaze swung to hers and back to the fire before he poked at it again. "I'm sorry. My comment was inappropriate. You're right, I'm overtired." He jabbed the poker into one of the logs, shooting sparks up the chimney and onto the slate hearth under his knees.

"Josephine had me fooled," he said. "Her family's paying the biggest price, though."

"I feel sorry for them."

"I suspect most folks do." He turned from the fireplace and took the chair at the desk. "I'm glad you're here. About my sermon on Sunday. It's why I came to find you on Thursday at Miss Sophie's."

In all the excitement of the last two days, Isabelle had forgotten about his arrival on Miss Sophie's doorstep. Her body tensed. His sermon? Of course he wanted to talk about his sermon. Why wouldn't he want to reiterate how "all have sinned"? As if she didn't already know. But Jesus had forgiven her. Isabelle raised her chin. "I'm not interested in your sermon."

Preach swiped through his hair, smoothing some of the clumps. "You're not interested in what part of my sermon?"

"Hearing you remind me about how much I've sinned."

Preach's chest deflated as if she'd punched him.

It was time for Isabelle to take her leave. He could hear from the others about her departure with her father. Aunt Lou could tell Preach herself if she cared so much about him.

"Snoop was right."

Isabelle's hand slipped from the door latch. *Snoop* thought Isabelle was a sinner? The room echoed with her sharp laugh as she turned back to face Preach. "Don't you think that's the pot calling the kettle black?"

"Snoop was a lot of things: a thief, a cheat, a liar. But he was also perceptive. Give him time, he could figure almost anything out. He's the one who told me about you."

Isabelle drew a deliberate breath through her nose to avoid the quaking of her voice. "About me? What was there to tell about me that you didn't already know? You, however, hold all kinds of secrets, Mr. Preacher. It was Snoop who told me I should ask about Lavinia." It was cruel to bring the woman up now, when Isabelle was planning to leave, but, dropping her volume, she pressed on. "So I guess I'm asking, who's Lavinia?"

He slid both palms down his flushed cheeks before speaking. "Isabelle, I've done a lot of things in my life I'm not proud of. Before I met the Lord, when we had time off, I was always the first one up to the bar and more often than not the brothel. There was one woman in particular, Lavinia. I knew Snoop was partial to her, but I wanted to get back at him. I spent some time with her just so I could hurt Snoop. He's never let me forget it."

The pages of Preach's Bible crinkled as he smoothed them. "I'm beginning to realize, it's not about forgetting the sin, it's about remembering the Lord. Believing in the Lord has changed me on the inside. I don't have to do those things anymore."

Of course there would have been other women in Preach's life. The revelation still unsettled her heart. *Lord, help me to forgive.*

"I'd like to tell you I'm not tempted to sin, but I'm tempted every day to return to my old ways. Which brings me around to my sermon."

Enough, Preach.

"I wasn't trying to remind you of how much you'd sinned."

Isabelle stared at the fire. "It sure felt that way after what I'd shared with you."

"That's what Snoop told me. He said you'd taken my sermon personally. But the point of my sermon was not 'For all have sinned...' It was the next verse, Romans 3:24. 'Being justified freely by his grace through the redemption that is in Christ Jesus.' I wanted people to remember our sins are redeemed by the gracious forgiveness found in Jesus Christ."

Why didn't he understand? Sorrow welled up in her heart as she whispered, "Unless, of course, one already knows the Lord."

"What?"

"It sounds to me like you're preaching that your sins are forgiven because you committed them before you knew the Lord, but I have to carry the loss of my innocence my entire life, and it wasn't even my fault."

Isabelle pressed her eyes to slow the spring of tears.

∾

*I*sabelle's words gripped Preach's throat like a vice. She was right. He had kept himself from admitting how much he cared for her because of what Daniel had done. In his desire to appear more respectable, Preach had declared Isabelle unworthy to be his wife, even though she had every quality he admired: kindness, honesty, generosity, intelligence…

He rose from his chair and rounded the desk to kneel on one knee in front of Isabelle. Sobs shook her narrow shoulders. "Shhhh." He drew her hands from her face. With one thumb, he gathered the tears under each eye before taking her trembling hands in his own. "Isabelle, I'm sorry. I've been a judgmental fool. You're right. I've treated you like you're covered in some sort of shameful tarnish that can't be rubbed off. It's not fair. Jesus made you as pure and white as sheep's wool."

Isabelle lifted her gaze to his. Delicate beads of moisture flecked her lashes. She'd never looked more beautiful.

"The truth is, I fell for you the first day we met down by the creek. And since then, I've only grown to love you more, even if I was too stubborn to admit it." Preach leaned close enough for Isabelle's warm breaths to caress his cheeks. He swallowed. "You are the only woman I've ever wished to spend the rest of my life with. Would you consider becoming my bride?"

Preach pressed his lips to Isabelle's forehead and then each eyelid before hovering over her mouth.

She leaned forward until her soft lips touched his.

The kiss was just like he'd imagined it would be—sweet, breathtaking. Preach's heart hammered against his ribs as he wrapped his arms around Isabelle's shoulders.

Isabelle sighed and burrowed her head against the collar of his shirt.

"Is that a yes?"

EPILOGUE

*I*sabelle tugged at the delicate ivory chiffon at her wrists before adjusting the folds. Mother had done a remarkable job, working with her seamstress, to fashion such a pretty gown in one month's time. Raising her eyes to the elegant dressing mirror in Miss Sophie's guest room, Isabelle smoothed the layers of silk in the floor-length skirt accentuating her returning curves.

Kittie's reflection appeared in the mirror as she tidied the deep folds of lace cascading from the wide satin sash at Isabelle's shoulders. "You couldn't be more beautiful." Kittie planted a kiss on Isabelle's cheek.

"Do you think so?"

An imprint of lips from Kittie's red lip salve blazed on Isabelle's cheek. "Kittie. Look what you've done."

Kittie tittered as Isabelle swiped at her cheek, smearing the salve into two long streaks down her face.

"I don't think that's helping." Kittie's shoulders quaked with mirth.

"Please, you have to remove it." Isabelle rubbed her cheek

again, smearing the salve even further. "I look like a clown." Preach deserved so much more.

"An attractive clown on her wedding day." Kittie's laughter bubbled over as she snatched a hankie from the chiffonier and scooped up some cold cream. "Hold still." She dabbed Isabelle's nose and left a stark white blob at its tip.

Isabelle stared at her reflection for a brief moment before joining Kittie in her mirth. Soon the two were bent over, clutching their stomachs and giggling.

Just like old times in Isabelle's bedroom at home.

Two raps sounded on the door before Aunt Lou issued a warning. "It's time to leave for the church."

Isabelle clutched her best friend's hand in her own. "Kittie, I'm so grateful you could be here as my maid of honor."

"Wild horses couldn't have kept me away. I'm happy you've found someone who truly loves you. Now let me fix your beautiful face."

Someone who truly loved her and was patient, kind, good, and gentle.

Ten minutes later, Archie, the Franklin family's driver, pulled the carriage to a stop in front of the Stony Creek Chapel. Alexander led his wife and sister inside before returning to escort Isabelle and Kittie to the narrow vestibule.

Isabelle tightened her grip on her large bouquet. Within the sphere of purple cloth roses and off-white looped ribbons perched the second sparrow Preach had carved. *Lord, thank you for teaching me I don't have to be afraid and for caring for me as you care for the sparrows. I promise to love the wonderful man you've given to me and to help him care for your people the rest of my life.*

∽

*P*reach shifted on his feet as he waited at the front of the church beside Samuel Gittens, the itinerant minister who'd led him to the Lord. The black wool suit he'd ordered from the general store pulled across Preach's shoulders. His back was on fire. The sooner he could be out of the church and in the freezing temperatures of November, the better.

Thinking the way he did, it probably wouldn't be long before the Stony Creek Chapel regretted the decision they'd made to keep him on as pastor.

A small group of congregants, headed by Miss Sophie, had arrived at the camp shortly after he'd let the elders know he was quitting. Miss Sophie had gone on at length about how much the people needed him and how the funeral for Horace had touched so many lives. Her words had come as a surprise. His mind had been muddled during the service, knowing that Isabelle had agreed to marry him the night before. Preach had tried to convince the group he wasn't fit to lead others toward the Lord when Miss Sophie had said humility was a good quality in a preacher.

After her comment, Preach had agreed to continue on as their pastor until he and Isabelle left the camp at spring break-up.

Preach had also tried to convince Isabelle to let him set her up in a little house in town until then, but she wouldn't hear of it. She'd insisted that, as his wife, her place was by his side always and not just on weekends.

Isabelle had asked Aunt Lou to keep her on as assistant cook, and she'd agreed. Joe had offered his quarters to the couple and moved into the bunkhouse with the other men. Perley was already taking bets on how long it would take Joe to find better accommodations.

Fidgeting in the third pew caught Preach's eye. Lewis was

jabbing Mack in the ribs. The two youngsters had gotten into no end of trouble since Mack had recuperated from his illness.

Will sat next to the two, immobile. Horace's death seemed to have set the young man adrift. It was as if he didn't care about anything anymore. Against Preach's advice, Ernie had agreed to take Will on the spring river drive to deliver Pollitt's logs to the West Pine Timber Company down river. The money was good, but the work was dangerous, particularly when you were young and foolish. Preach hoped Ernie knew what he was doing. Will's family didn't need any more loss.

At a signal from Isabelle's Father, Phyllis struck up Pachelbel's "Canon in D." When she'd learned of Isabelle's and Preach's engagement, Phyllis had offered to play the piano for their ceremony. She'd also apologized for her daughter's traitorous behavior. No one in town had heard from either Snoop or Josephine since their escape a month earlier, and the Thorebourne family home had gone up for sale to help cover the timber company's loss.

As the delicate notes drifted through the sanctuary, Isabelle's friend Kittie began her walk up the aisle. Preach gulped at the vision behind Kitty walking toward him on her father's arm. Isabelle looked like a fairytale princess, her hair all piled up, a sort of diamond crown on her head. He was the most fortunate man in the world. *Lord, I thank you that the woman you've chosen for me is beautiful both inside and out.*

Preach's heart danced as Alexander presented his daughter's hand. Preach nodded his gratitude before slipping Isabelle's tiny glove through the crook of his elbow. Her calm smile brought a surge of emotion to his throat.

Together, they turned to face Samuel, the man who would unite them before God and all those present for the rest of their lives.

Did you enjoy this book? We hope so!
Would you take a quick minute to leave a review where you purchased the book?
It doesn't have to be long. Just a sentence or two telling what you liked about the story!

~

Receive a FREE ebook and get updates when new Wild Heart books release: https://www.wildheartbooks.org/newsletter

Don't miss *Rocky Mountain Revelation*, book 2 in the Rocky Mountain Revival series!

Chapter One

1898

The Rocky Mountains

A sharp squeal pierced the air, followed by a dull thud. Will tightened his grip on the tin cup of coffee he'd been nursing for half an hour and looked to his left. Was someone in trouble?

Mack shot out of the cook tent. Tight on his heels ran a woman—or perhaps *girl* was more appropriate—a long black braid coursing down her back.

With a cast iron frying pan raised in one arm, she chased Mack toward the trees. "You're going to regret that!"

"I already do," Mack said over one shoulder and rubbed the top of his head before he stretched the gap between himself and his angry pursuer.

Will's gaze moved to the man, who looked around his pa's age, perched across from him on the six-foot half-log deacon seat beside the crackling campfire. His stomach clenched. The man *would* be around his pa's age, if Pa were still alive. "You figure those two are going to be all right?" Will thrust his chin toward the opening in the pines where Mack appeared to be aiming.

For the first time that morning, the brim of the older man's wool cap lifted, and his dark brown eyes bore into Will's. "I 'spect so." The reply was more of a grumble than actual words.

The last of the girl's white apron strings disappeared into the forest. He tossed his cold coffee onto the ground. The vile stuff still hadn't grown on him. He uncrossed his long legs and stood to follow Mack and the girl.

"You know that boy?"

Mack was a year older than Will, and they'd just finished their first season chopping for Pollitt's Lumber up on Cougar Ridge Mountain near the town of Stony Creek. They'd been thrilled to be taken on for a spring river drive in the Rocky Mountains. The log drive would deliver Pollitt's, and several other companies', winter season's logs to the West Pine Timber Company downstream.

Preach, the foreman over at Pollitt's, had given Mack and Will a fine recommendation to join the drive. Will still wasn't sure if he deserved it or if Preach simply felt sorry for him. "Ya, I know him."

"I imagine there's a reason your friend was recommended." Mack was scrawny, no doubt. Will carried more meat on him, but Mack's agility and stamina would hold up in the long days and hard work of the drive.

"He can probably manage his current predicament," the stranger said. "Don't you figure?"

Will's gaze drifted back to the woods. The man had a point. The girl was just a slip of a thing, and Mack usually deserved any grief he acquired. The boy was relentless in playing practical jokes.

Will resumed his place before the fire. "My name's Will. I don't think we've met." Not that they'd met anyone yet. Mack and he had arrived at Isaac Lake the afternoon before. Since then, they'd spent most of their time in the tent sleeping off the couple of days they'd caroused in Stony Creek to celebrate the last payday of the logging season.

The pay was one of the reasons Will found the log drive appealing. He stood to make two dollars a day for three weeks. It would go a long way to cover his recent loss. He'd been rolled the last evening in town, and the entire month's pay had gone to a pretty face with some fast fingers. Now that pa was dead, Will's ma depended on her three sons to take care of the family. Eight mouths were a lot to feed.

"They call me Gabe," the older man said. "It's nice to meet you, son."

Will gritted his teeth to keep the term from twisting his features. No one had called him son since Pa's death last fall.

Gabe leaned back and snatched up a branch of spruce from a pile of deadfall behind the deacon seat. He shoved one end under a cogged leather boot, snapped the branch in two, and tossed them into the fire.

The fire cracked and popped as it consumed the new fuel.

Will swallowed to steady his voice before he spoke. If he took his time, it wouldn't squeak like it usually did when his emotions were churning. The last thing Will needed on the river drive was for the men to think he was some kind of punk. At seventeen, he might well be the youngest, but folks said he looked older than his years. Will straightened his shoulders, "You have any idea when we might be heading out?"

"More than likely in the next day or two. It's expensive to keep feeding the drivers if they're not working."

If river drivers ate anything like loggers, piles of food stuffs disappeared in minutes. It would take a lot for the drive's cook to beat Lou Franklin's cooking in such primitive conditions.

She and her niece Isabelle had kept Pollitt's men well supplied with cookies, pies, and—Will's personal favorite—Lou's raisin cake. "The cook any good?"

Gabe huffed and sipped his coffee.

Steam spiraled up, obscuring the deep crevasses lining his face, crevasses earned by spending a lot of years out of doors.

"Shorty is one of the best. He won't be too happy your friend ran off with his assistant. He's got a lot of men to feed."

Will thought of the young woman who'd chased Mack out of the tent, her dark eyes snapping. Tall and willowy, like his eldest sister, Vesta, the girl's heart-shaped face and narrow pointed chin held a determination Mack would be unlikely to outrun. "Seems like an unusual job for a girl that young."

Gabe's eyes combed Will's as the heat built up under his collar. It was a dumb thing to say considering Will's own tender years. He lifted the gray wool cap covering his shoulder-length blond hair and slicked through the curls before he returned the hat to his head and cinched it low on his brow.

Ernie, a fellow logger from Pollitt's Lumber, had taken Mack and Will under his wing after he learned they were working the drive together. He had also crushed Mack's hopes of a romantic entanglement when he'd informed him the same rules applied on the river drive as in the lumber camp—no single women allowed.

"She married?" Will asked and chuckled at his own humor. There was no way a girl that young—

"Widowed."

The information caught in Will's throat, he bent to cough as Gabe took another sip of his coffee.

"Widowed?" Will's voice squeaked. Drat! He coughed again. Maybe Gabe would think Will had something in his throat.

"No more than two months. She's still hurting. The drive will keep her busy enough and that should help."

Spending time in the woods with a rowdy bunch of men was

not the best choice for a grieving heart. He should know. More than likely the drive would find the girl another man to marry if she wanted one. It wouldn't be Will, though. He was too young to be tied down. And he wasn't particularly fond of having his noggin bashed with a frying pan either. "It's a sad thing." Will lowered his chin, hoping his face held the appropriate amount of sympathy to fit the poor girl's loss.

Gabe rose from the fire. "I'm going for a walk before break-fast. You care to come along?"

Will looked to the break in the trees where Mack and the girl had vanished. There was still no sign of the couple. It would feel good to stretch his legs and take his mind off his rumbling stomach. Breakfast wasn't for another half hour. "Sure, I'll come with ya."

Gabe's tin cup clanked on the bottom of the white enameled dish tub, when Will and he passed the canvas cook tent. Curs-ing, muttered under a man's breath, followed Gabe and Will as they stepped into the shade of evergreens no more than thirty feet tall, interspersed with flat topped stumps. The sharp musk of the forest wafted on the air. Branches snapped under their feet with every step as they hiked.

They'd been hiking in silence for ten minutes when Will asked, "Do you know when the area was logged off?"

"My pa, my brothers, and I logged here in seventy-eight. I wasn't much older than you."

Will stared at the back of Gabe's broad Mackinaw jacket, the red-and-black plaid a bold contrast to the emerald of the forest. "That would have made you about..."

Looking over his shoulder, Gabe shot Will a retort. "Eighteen."

Will couldn't help the disappointed grunt that escaped his chest. The girls in town had been lying to him for six months. "All right, you got me figured. I'm only seventeen, but that doesn't mean I can't put in a man's worth of work."

"Did you hear me say you couldn't?"

Several jays took flight, the flap of their wings overhead, as Will lengthened his stride to catch up with Gabe. "I was a chopping over at Pollitt's with my pa until…" Telling Gabe Will was the reason his pa was dead wasn't going to bolster Gabe's opinion of him, but Pa deserved for Will to admit what he'd done. Gabe stopped and rotated to face Will.

Will's chest heaved as he attempted to slow his breath.

Raising a heavy dark eyebrow, Gabe placed his hands on his hips. "Until?"

Even though Will could only thank himself for bringing the topic up, it didn't make the telling any easier. He lifted his cap and ran his fingers through his hair. Preach and the other loggers had been trying to convince Will it wasn't his fault ever since Pa had died, but it hadn't taken root. "I hate to say it." Will swallowed the bile rising in his throat. "Until I killed him."

Gabe's eyes took on a look of flint. "Are you telling me you killed your own pa?"

"I didn't raise my hand to him, but I might as well have. Last October, he and I had already met our quota by early afternoon. I guess it went to our heads, and we figured we could fall a sidewinder." The next words caught in Will's throat. "I was wedging the blasted thing when she blew. The doc told Preach Pa didn't feel a thing, but it doesn't make him any less dead."

Gabe grabbed Will's shoulder with wide fingers and squeezed. "I suspect your foreman told you the logging business is dangerous. You didn't know it was going to happen."

Will dropped his chin to his chest. "You can't hold yourself responsible."

Preach had said those exact words. Hearing them from Gabe didn't make them feel any more true.

Gabe gave Will's shoulder a final squeeze before he resumed his trek through the woods.

Several minutes later they arrived at a narrow stream. The

water rushed over the rocks, and debris heaped on its bed. After bending a willow branch, Gabe let the length of it slide through his fingers and inspected the buds at its tip.

Will stepped onto the smooth stones that lined the stream and scooped water to his lips. The frigid liquid, straight from the mountain's top, slid down his throat and soothed some of the ache caused by rehashing Pa's death. Will slurped down another scoop before he stepped onto the bank.

Gabe was sifting a thumb through several poplar catkins curled on his palm. He studied them for a moment before he lifted his gaze upstream.

"You looking for anything in particular?"

"Nope. We'll cross on over to Harper's Creek on our way back. How are your feet?"

Will wiggled his toes inside his Bass boots, known in the area to be the best footwear for river drives. The movement renewed a burn on his heels. Any man worth his salt could tell the boots were brand new and more than likely causing the wearer considerable pain. "They're not too bad. I'll be fine."

"You sure about that?"

Will didn't need the men on the log drive pampering him as they had over at Pollitt's. It was time Will Matheson became a man. "I *said* I'll be fine."

Drawing his brows together, Gabe looked Will over as if he didn't believe him.

Who did Gabe think he was, anyway?

"Talk to Noah before we head out. He's got a tin of rub he swears by, if you can stand the smell of the stuff. It'll make your boots waterproof and soften them up some." Gabe headed back the way they'd come.

At Harper's Creek, he surveyed the banks and checked the buds on the willow, cottonwood, and alder trees like some kind of nature fanatic before they returned to the camp. As the white of the cook tent came into view, Gabe sent Will on to breakfast and claimed he'd eat later in the day.

"The cook stands for that? Men chowing down whenever they want?" The only time Lou interfered with the meal schedule at Pollitt's was when the whole bunkhouse was down with hand, foot, and mouth. If a man tried to sneak into the kitchen between meals, he was likely to get a hot dipper of water thrown at him or, at the very least, a straw broom warming his backside.

Gabe chuckled as if he recalled some private joke. "I don't suppose Shorty does. You enjoy your breakfast."

Will rounded the cook tent. Beside the fire, tin plates and forks in their grip, sat a motley crew of about fifteen men destined to be either his good friends or his bad enemies. Every one of them wore the typical garb of Mackinaw jacket, Humphrey pants, and leather caulked boots.

The only men Will could be certain about were the ones who had come over from Pollitt's with him. Ernie, who'd assigned himself as Mack and Will's keeper, and Perley, gambler extraordinaire.

It wouldn't be an exaggeration to say Perley would risk losing his own mother if the odds appeared in his favor. As it was, he didn't look like himself, owing to the fact that he'd lost a wager while the Pollitt's crew caroused in Stony Creek. The loss required the shearing of the long brown hair he'd grown through the winter, and of which he'd been particularly proud. Unfortunately, the lack of hair made his beak of a nose and wide lips more prominent than usual.

Perley swung an arm over his head and motioned Will toward the fire. "It's about time you woke up. I was about to come looking for you and Mack— after breakfast that is."

Several men in the vicinity guffawed, raising the hackles on Will's back. Mack made a nuisance of himself with all his horsing around, but he never meant it in a mean-spirited way.

The same couldn't be said of Perley. He loved to get under your skin like a tick, and once he was there, it was hard to shake him lose.

"I was drinking coffee at sunup."

Perley's eyes widened. *"You* were drinking coffee?"

More like holding a full mug to keep his hands warm, but Will wasn't going to admit the fact. If being a man meant you had to like coffee, he'd learn to like it.

"Where's your better half then?" Perley asked.

The man to Perley's right snorted before he twisted the corners of his manicured mustache. The last thing Perley needed was somebody who egged him on. Perley bobbed his head to his neighbor. "The boys are a couple of young boomers our push sent over. I'm not sure what he saw in them. I don't imagine they'll last long."

The two cackled like a couple of old hens.

If Perley wasn't a head taller than Will's five foot eleven, he might take a swing at him. It was Mack and Will's first river drive, but they meant to prove their worth. It wasn't as if Perley had much to brag about, it was only his second year on the drive.

The jangle of the breakfast gong interrupted Will's irritation. Like a bunch of school children running for recess, the crew raced to the makeshift table outside the cook tent.

Will followed several lengths behind. Where in tarnation was Mack?

The men fell into an orderly line and heaped flapjacks, fried ham, and eggs onto their plates out of large enameled tubs. The majority also poured a thick layer of corn syrup from a galvanized pitcher over their plate's contents before they returned to their seats beside the fire.

When the white bottom of the flapjack basin peaked through, one of the men called for the cook. Will struggled to keep his mouth from flopping open as the smallest man he had ever seen whisked out of the cook tent.

No higher than Will's chest, the cook's slender frame and delicate shoulders looked out of place hauling a basin full to the brim with flapjacks. "Get out of my way," he said with a surprisingly low voice as he shouldered a path through men anxious to fill their plates. The cook's droopy brown mustache quivered with the effort.

"Shorty, there's no need to be ornery," one of the men growled back. "We're hungry."

Shorty replaced the empty tub of flapjacks with the full tub before he thrust his chin toward the speaker. "I wouldn't be so ornery if someone hadn't taken off with my helper more than half an hour ago. You know how much effort it takes to feed you ruffians?"

In unfortunate timing, Mack and the girl appeared at a gap in the trees, and the men started up a ruckus of hooting and hollering. Mack, a hangdog look about him, followed the girl, who wore a black halo of mussed hair about her face.

Shorty marched toward the pair, shouting a string of curses blue enough to turn Will's throat red.

The girl's boots grabbed the dirt not two paces from Shorty. Her chin flicked up.

"I'm of half a mind to fire you," Shorty said.

"You just try." The words shot from her mouth like a warning.

Shorty leaned sideways to peer around the girl and stared up at Mack. "Until we head out on the river, you've got yourself a job—cook's second helper. That means you listen to me and her." Shorty shook a pointer finger at Mack. "And if I have to raise my voice, even once, to find you, you'll be the body they never discover at the bottom of the lake. Follow me." Shorty whirled around and headed back to the cook tent, the girl and Mack in his wake.

Perley's voice could be heard above the other voices drifting from the campfire. "She's a fine piece of calico." He sucked air between his teeth and tongue.

Will gaze returned to the girl who followed Shorty. In spite of her disarray, the features Will had observed earlier fell together to make a particularly pretty picture. Perley had no business noticing, though. A girl that young and sweet looking, her attack on Mack aside, was much too good for the likes of man with Perley's predilections.

GET FOR *ROCKY MOUNTAIN REVELATION* AT YOUR FAVORITE RETAILER.

GET ALL THE BOOKS IN THE ROCKY MOUNTAIN REVIVAL SERIES

Book 1: Rocky Mountain Redemption

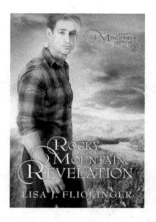

Book 2: Rocky Mountain Revelation

ABOUT THE AUTHOR

Lisa J. Flickinger lives and writes from the cliff of a river along the majestic Rocky Mountains. When not writing or reading, you will find her scouring antique shops or sipping a maple latte with friends and family.

To learn more about her other books, visit http://lisajflickinger.com/.

ACKNOWLEDGMENTS

My thanks go to Larry, lumberjack and story teller extraordinaire. I appreciate your inspiration to write about life in the old lumber camps.

Thanks also go to Robin Patchen, editor of *Rocky Mountain Redemption* and *Rocky Mountain Revelation*. Your ability to see things in a manuscript I can't see inspires me.

Special acknowledgement goes to Misty M. Beller of Wild Heart Books. Thanks so much for believing in my stories and giving me the opportunity to join your authors.

I'm deeply indebted to my husband Matt who puts up with all the nonsense of writing, editing, re-editing, re-re-editing...

If you love historical romance, check out the other Wild Heart books!

Marisol ~ Spanish Rose by Elva Cobb Martin

Escaping to the New World is her only option...Rescuing her will wrap the chains of the Inquisition around his neck.

Marisol Valentin flees Spain after murdering the nobleman who molested her. She ends up for sale on the indentured servants' block at Charles Town harbor—dirty, angry, and with child. Her hopes are shattered, but she must find a refuge for herself and the child she carries. Can this new land offer her the grace, love, and security she craves? Or must she escape again to her only living relative in Cartagena?

Captain Ethan Becket, once a Charles Town minister, now sails the seas as a privateer, grieving his deceased wife. But when he takes captive a ship full of indentured servants, he's intrigued by the woman whose manners seem much more refined than the average Spanish serving girl. Perfect to become governess for his young son. But when he sets out on a quest to find his captured sister, said to be in Cartagena, little does he expect his new Spanish governess to stow away on his ship with her six-month-old son. Yet her offer of help to free his sister is too tempting to pass up. And her beauty, both inside and out, is too attractive for his heart to protect itself against—until he learns she is a wanted murderess.

As their paths intertwine on a journey filled with danger, intrigue, and romance, only love and the grace of God can overcome the past and ignite a new beginning for Marisol and Ethan.

~

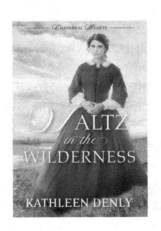

Waltz in the Wilderness by Kathleen Denly

She's desperate to find her missing father. His conscience demands he risk all to help.

Eliza Brooks is haunted by her role in her mother's death, so she'll do anything to find her missing pa—even if it means sneaking aboard a southbound ship. When those meant to protect her abandon and betray her instead, a family friend's unexpected assistance is a blessing she can't refuse.

Daniel Clarke came to California to make his fortune, and a stable job as a San Francisco carpenter has earned him more than most have scraped from the local goldfields. But it's been four years since he left Massachusetts and his fiancé is impatient for his return. Bound for home at last, Daniel Clarke finds his heart and plans challenged by a tenacious young woman with haunted eyes. Though every word he utters seems to offend her, he is determined to see her safely returned to her father. Even if that means risking his fragile engagement.

When disaster befalls them in the remote wilderness of the Southern California mountains, true feelings are revealed, and both must face heart-rending decisions. But how to decide when every choice before them leads to someone getting hurt?

~

Lone Star Ranger by Renae Brumbaugh Green

Elizabeth Covington will get her man.

And she has just a week to prove her brother isn't the murderer Texas Ranger Rett Smith accuses him of being. She'll show the good-looking lawman he's wrong, even if it means setting out on a risky race across Texas to catch the real killer.

Rett doesn't want to convict an innocent man. But he can't let the Boston beauty sway his senses to set a guilty man free. When Elizabeth follows him on a dangerous trek, the Ranger vows to keep her safe. But who will protect him from the woman whose conviction and courage leave him doubting everything—even his heart?

CPSIA information can be obtained
at www.ICGtesting.com
Printed in the USA
LVHW051957171220
674450LV00014B/1317